It was obvi... hadn't end... which mea... would be ab... ...as reversing the effects of global warming.

Emily had tried to forget him, but never quite managed to pull that off. Maybe because he'd fathered her baby.

The fact was they were both responsible for this child and he was determined to be a father, so she needed to find a path to peaceful coexistence. But moving in with him, relying on him, leaning on him—that was a path she wouldn't go down.

Cal smiled at Annie, who looked more curious than wary. "Is that a truce?"

"I think a cease-fire is an excellent idea," Em agreed.

She hoped she wouldn't regret those words. It would be so easy to fall in love with him....

Dear Reader,

When asked to participate in Special Edition's FAMOUS FAMILIES project, I was truly honored. It was fun to bring back characters from the MEN OF MERCY MEDICAL series, and it started me thinking about the meaning of family.

I'm one of six children, and my only sister passed away from melanoma, making my brothers and me appreciate each other even more. It's the family I was born into, but losing my sister makes me treasure my female friends, who are the sisters of my heart. People at the office or in the neighborhood become an extension of home. In hospitals, the personnel work as a unit to save lives.

The editorial staff at Silhouette Books have come to mean so much to me, as have the readers with whom I share a love of romance. It's a connection that makes us family and we rock.

I sincerely hope you enjoy Cal and Emily's story as they fall in love and make a family with their little girl.

All the best,

Teresa Southwick

TERESA SOUTHWICK

The Doctor's Secret Baby

SPECIAL EDITION

Published by Silhouette Books

America's Publisher of Contemporary Romance

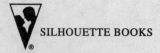

SILHOUETTE BOOKS

ISBN-13: 978-0-373-65464-2

Recycling programs
for this product may
not exist in your area.

THE DOCTOR'S SECRET BABY

Printed in U.S.A.

Books by Teresa Southwick

TERESA SOUTHWICK

lives with her husband in Las Vegas, the city that reinvents itself every day. An avid fan of romance novels, she is delighted to be living out her dream of writing for Silhouette Books.

To Gail Chasan and Charles Griemsman,
my Silhouette Special Edition family. You make it a joy
to work at what I love best, writing romance.

Chapter One

Telling an old boyfriend he had a daughter he didn't know about was a crappy way to start the day.

And the emergency room at Mercy Medical Center where he was working was a crappy place to tell him, but Emily Summers knew for sure she could find him there. Dr. Cal Westen was a pediatric emergency specialist and would be on duty shortly. He always stopped in the E.R. break room for a cup of coffee about thirty minutes before the start of his shift. At least he used to. She didn't know squat about his routine since they'd split up more than a year ago.

Emily opened the door and her heart skipped and skidded when she saw him. Some things didn't change, including her profound physical reaction to this charismatic, charming doctor.

"Hi," she said, lifting a hand in greeting.

His grin when he saw her was instantaneous. "Emily Summers, as I live and breathe."

"Guilty." In so many ways, she thought. She moved farther into the room, just beside the rectangular, metal-framed folding table in the center of the room. It was littered with the daily newspaper. The flat-screen TV was tuned to a news channel with the ticker scrolling across the bottom. "How are you, Cal?"

"Good."

He looked good. But then he always had—tall, tan, muscular. The man even made his shapeless blue scrubs look as sexy as sin. Her past had a history of attraction to tall, dark and handsome guys, but two years ago Cal had made her rethink that. His sandy hair was short and gel-rumpled in a calculated Hollywood-heartthrob way, but had probably cost him about thirty seconds. A deep dimple softened his square jaw.

"It's good to see you." Dark blue eyes twinkled with genuine pleasure, but after she told him what she had to say, he'd rethink that. He straightened away from the counter and set his paper cup on the table still separating them. "Can I buy you a cup of coffee?"

"No, thanks." She was already jittery enough. And what with the adrenaline surging through her, caffeine might just implode her heart. Maybe the E.R. was the right place to deliver her news after all.

"How long has it been?" he asked.

Because she'd been four weeks into her first trimester the last time she'd seen him and her life since then had passed in a blur of pregnancy and baby months, she knew exactly how long ago it was since she'd last seen him. "Just shy of two years."

"Seems like yesterday," he said, shaking his head.

For her, it hardly seemed like that, because her life had been altered so profoundly in their time apart. From the first moment the infant had moved inside her, she'd felt a love bigger than anything she'd ever felt before. And when she'd held her baby for the first time, she knew that giving up her life to protect her child wouldn't be too big a sacrifice.

Her little girl was the only reason she'd come here today because seeing Cal again was the last thing she wanted to do. She'd broken things off after he broke her heart.

He looked her over from head to toe and smiled. "Your hair is shorter."

"I cut it. Easier this way," she said, touching a hand to her short, shiny bob. A typical guy, he'd always liked her brown hair long.

"Looks good. Really good." There was approval in his eyes. "Have you lost weight?"

"Always the charmer," she said. During her first trimester, morning sickness had taken a toll and the rest of the pregnancy had been only marginally better. Life since giving birth had kept her busy and she hadn't regained the twelve pounds lost from her five-feet-two-inch height. The denim capris she had on were several sizes smaller than anything he'd seen her in—or out of. "I might have dropped a little weight."

"Seriously, there's something different."

She'd had a baby—his baby—but didn't want to blurt that out. Although why she should be concerned about his feelings when he'd decimated hers was a mystery. "I'm still the same."

Studying her, he folded his arms over his chest, drawing her attention to the broad contour of muscle. It seemed like yesterday that she'd run her hands over the coarse dusting of hair that she remembered being darker than what grew on his head, more reddish brown. The memory made her heart kick up again like it had so many times before when they'd been together.

He moved around the table and stopped in front of her,

close enough to feel the heat from his body. "You look great, Em. What's your secret?"

"Oh, you know…" She shrugged.

"I never heard where you went when you left Mercy Medical Center."

Did that mean he'd tried to find out? Just when she'd thought her heart was under control, it stuttered again, a completely involuntary reaction because there was no way she'd react like this to him of her own free will. She never wanted to hurt again the way he'd made her hurt.

"I went to Sunrise Medical Center."

"Still a social worker?" he asked.

"Yes. And a few other things."

He nodded. "Whatever you're doing certainly agrees with you."

Being a mom? It was something she'd wanted since her very first pregnancy, and having the baby she'd been too young to have. Giving that child to another mother to care for had left an empty place inside her that had been impossible to fill.

"How've you been, Cal?" she asked, still procrastinating.

"Great."

Was there a little too much enthusiasm in his tone? Or was it wishful thinking that he was working at convincing her he'd been fine since they split?

"How've you been, Em?"

It was a segue, and she might as well go with it. She couldn't put this off any longer. "Funny you should ask…"

"What?" he asked, frowning.

When he reached out and touched her, his big hand felt too good, too warm, too safe. Static filled her head as electricity arced through her body. She stepped back and blew out a long breath.

"I have a lump in my breast," she said.

Concern turned to worry in his expression. All at once he wasn't her ex, but a doctor. "There's no reason to assume the worst. Have you seen someone?"

"I have an appointment, but—"

"Lindquist is a breast specialist. I know him pretty well. I'll give him a call and get you in right away—"

"No."

"Em, you can't put it off."

"You said there's no reason to assume the worst." Even though that's exactly what she'd done and why she was here in the first place.

"And I stand by that. But why worry any longer than necessary?"

"I'm taking care of that. And it's not really what I wanted to talk to you about."

"There's more?" Now he looked confused and concerned and she couldn't blame him.

"Finding the lump made me think long and hard about my own mortality," she said.

"You're young. There's no reason to borrow trouble."

She didn't have to borrow it. Trouble had a way of finding her. "I'm not concerned about myself." She took a deep breath and forced herself not to look away. "It's my baby."

"Baby? I didn't know—" He stopped as the dots started to connect.

"Our baby. She's eleven months old."

"She? A girl?"

Em nodded. "Her name is Ann Marie. Annie."

"Ann is my mother's middle name," he said, as if he couldn't think of anything else to say.

"Marie is my mother's middle name. It seemed fair." Even if it would never feel right after the choice her mother had forced on her.

He ran his fingers through his hair. "What the hell are you saying?"

The calm before the storm was over. "I'm telling you that you have a little girl."

"If I believed you—"

"If?" Now it was her turn to be shocked. The thought that he would question the facts had never occurred to her. At least not consciously. But somewhere deep inside she'd probably suspected. Otherwise she'd have called him instead of meeting face-to-face so that he could see she was telling the truth. Annie's future depended on it.

"Why should I believe you, Em? You were the one who walked away. And before you did, you never said a word about being pregnant."

"You never gave me a chance."

"It's my fault?" He held up his fingers. "Two words. *I'm pregnant.* That's all you had to say."

"It wasn't that easy." Not after that horrible time when she was little more than a child herself.

"For the sake of argument, I have to ask—why are you telling me now?"

"Because of the lump," she said, twisting her fingers together. "If something happened to me Annie would have no one. I couldn't stand that."

"So this is about you?"

"No, it's about our daughter."

His gaze narrowed as suspicion swirled in his eyes. "Why should I believe you after all this time? What are you after, Em? What do you want from me?"

Emily hadn't believed it was possible to hurt more than she had the night she'd tried to tell Cal Westen about his baby, but she was wrong. His second rejection was twice as painful because of Annie. How could he reject that sweet baby girl?

The innocent child who was depending on Em to take care of her. That's all she was trying to do in spite of what Cal thought.

"I was wrong not to tell you right away," she admitted.

"You think?" Sarcasm rippled between them.

"I'm hoping you won't punish your daughter for my mistake."

"There's no reason I should believe she's my daughter. I always used protection when we were together. It's not something I take for granted."

"Me, either," she said. That long-ago mistake made her pretty cautious. "I don't know what to tell you except I guess the condom broke."

At that moment Rhonda Levin walked in. Emily had seen the E.R. nurse manager from time to time when she worked here at Mercy Medical. The plump, brown-eyed, bleached blonde looked at each of them, narrowed her eyes, then settled her gaze on Cal.

"You're on, Doc. Paramedics are bringing in car accident victims. One of them is an eleven-month-old with head trauma. Whatever is going on here will have to wait. ETA, three minutes." Rhonda gave them a pointed look before walking out.

The baby coming in couldn't be in better hands, Emily thought. If it were her daughter there's no one she'd trust more than Cal. But he was looking at her now as if he didn't trust her as far as he could throw her.

"The condom broke? Come on, you can do better than that." Apparently he planned to use his three minutes to grill her.

"Did you read the directions? It's not guaranteed one hundred percent," she said.

"The percentage of security is in the high nineties," he shot back. "Again I have to ask why I should believe you're not trying to pass her off as mine."

Emily had pictured this scene in her mind and not once had

it included the part where he doubted Annie was his child. Now she knew how naive that was, because he was within his rights to question it. But tell that to the anger building up inside her.

She glared at him. "If you can ask me that, it's clear you never knew me at all. I'd never lie to you, Cal. Especially about something like this."

It felt like déjà vu all over again when she turned and walked out on him, but this time her heart was breaking for Annie, too.

Two days after Emily Summers had turned his life upside down, Cal sat in a booth at Coco's coffee shop on Eastern Avenue near the 215 Beltway and wondered whether she'd show up. If she'd changed her cell phone number he wouldn't have been able to contact her at all. She no longer lived at the address where—too many times to count—he'd picked her up for dinner and brought her back to make love to her. When she walked out on him, he'd missed her.

When she walked out on him again yesterday, he'd gone to work on that eleven-month-old. Fortunately the head trauma was superficial and the few stitches would eventually be covered by her hair and she'd probably have no memory of the ordeal. But he wasn't lucky enough to forget Emily's words: *Our baby.* She's eleven months old. He'd never known her to lie, and she'd looked sincerely surprised and angry that he hadn't believed her.

He took a sip of coffee and glanced at his watch for the umpteenth time. Eight-fifteen and almost dark outside. She'd picked the place—neutral territory—because she'd refused to give out her address. That implied a lack of trust, which was pretty ironic when you thought about it. She was passing her kid off as his and *he* couldn't be trusted?

Still, if there weren't doubts in his mind, he wouldn't have set up this meeting.

He looked up and saw Emily walking toward him. After all these months and this stunt she was trying to pull off, how could one look at that face tie him in knots? Her mouth was made to be kissed. Those full lips had turned him on more times than he could count and thoughts of running his hands through her dark, shiny hair had fueled more dreams than he wanted to admit.

She stopped by the table. "Cal."

"Have a seat." He indicated the booth bench across from him.

She was wearing a thin-strapped yellow tank and white capris. Her flip-flops matched her shirt and gave him an unobstructed view of her coral-painted toes. Sexiest feet in Vegas, he thought, again feeling stupid for the gut-level turn-on that he couldn't control. Apparently he hadn't outgrown his fatal flaw. Attraction to a deceitful woman had cost him big time and here he was again.

"So what did you want to talk about?" she asked. "You made your feelings pretty clear. As far as I'm concerned, there's nothing left to say."

"Maybe you don't think so, but I wasn't finished when you walked out the other day." He forced himself to relax his grip on the coffee mug in front of him. "Would you like something?"

"Just to get this over with." Her big brown eyes were defensive and still as beautiful as ever.

"Okay, then." He met her gaze and asked the question that had been gnawing at him since she'd left the E.R. "If she's my child—"

"Your daughter's name is Annie."

Without acknowledging that, he continued, "Why didn't you tell me I was going to be a father?"

She let out a breath and her gaze wandered out the window,

to the congestion of cars on Eastern, waiting to turn left onto the Beltway. It was cool inside, but he knew on the street it was still more than a hundred degrees. This was Vegas and it was July. Hot was a way of life. But hot didn't do justice to how he felt.

"Do you remember the last time we were together?" she asked, sliding into the place across from him.

"Yeah." Of course he did. "One minute everything was fine, the next you said we were done. A guy doesn't tend to forget something like that."

One corner of her mouth curved up, but not from amusement. "A guy like you doesn't forget because you're always the one who ends things. It was different with me and that bothered you."

The fact she was right didn't help. He liked women, and they returned the favor. He did end things before anyone got serious. So sue him. But with Em he hadn't been ready for things to be over.

"It came out of left field." That's all he'd admit.

Her eyes looked big and brown. Innocent and hurt. "Were you there for the last conversation we had?"

Maybe. "Refresh my memory."

"I know how you feel about commitment."

"We never talked about it," he protested.

Her expression was heavy on the scorn. "Every woman at Mercy Medical Center and probably the Las Vegas metropolitan area knows you don't make promises."

"Being a doctor is a demanding profession."

"I'm not talking about dinner and a show on Saturday night. Your aversion to responsibility, liability, obligation or dedication on a long-term basis is legendary. You're as shallow as a cookie sheet."

"That's harsh."

"But true. I knew that when we first went out. I was fine with it. I didn't want anything permanent, either. It worked as well for me as it did for you. Maybe more."

"So what was this conversation we had?"

"All I said was—wouldn't you like to have children someday? You're a pediatrician, and it's not a stretch to assume that you might want to have one of your own."

"Okay." He vaguely remembered.

"Do you recall your response?"

"Not in detail."

"I do." Shadows made her eyes darken even more. "You did five minutes straight on what *wasn't* going to happen. And I quote, 'Nothing could compel me to ever tie myself down in any way. If you want to get on the commitment train, I'll see you off at the station.' You told me you never wanted strings. In a fairly firm and deep voice you added, 'There's no set of circumstances known to man that could make me change my mind.'"

Ouch. Yeah, he remembered now. The speech should be familiar since he'd given it so many times. "Okay."

Frowning, she tipped her head, studying him as if he was an alien from another world. "I was trying to gently bring up the fact that I was pregnant. Your stay-single-or-perish soliloquy didn't exactly make it feel safe to do that."

"It's not about comfort. It's about what was right. Maybe I was a jerk—"

"Maybe?"

He ignored that. "Any time after that you could have called, dropped me a line, left a message on the answering machine. Something to the effect—'Cal, I'm going to have a baby. Thought you should know. Catch you later.'"

It wouldn't be the first time a woman tried to manipulate him by lobbing the pregnancy bomb. One that turned out to be a lie, the first of many before it had finally ended.

Emily looked small and tense in the big booth across from him. He couldn't see her hands, they were in her lap. He remembered that when she was nervous, she twisted her fingers together. Peeking under the table to see if that had changed wasn't happening.

"In your world—a man's world—that would be the way. But not in mine. You made it clear how you felt and there was no way I was going to burden my baby with a father who didn't want her."

Sounded pretty cold when she said it like that. "You didn't give me a chance to react with all the facts. If I'd known you were pregnant, we could have talked about it—"

"You talked. I listened and got the message. So shoot me for not wanting to hear any more."

"Until now," he reminded her, his gaze sliding to her breasts.

"Yeah." She shifted her shoulders as if to relieve the tension and keep from shattering. "When I found the lump, it forced me to go to the bad place and think about what would become of Annie without me." She met his gaze. "Her biological father—commitment-phobe and all—is the lesser of two evils."

"Careful, flattery like that will turn my head." The words oozed sarcasm because her low opinion of him rankled.

He was a stand-up guy; he saved lives every day. Some women actually called him a hero. Emily wasn't one of them. The lesser of two evils is still evil.

"Look, Cal—" She settled her hands on the table, twisting her fingers together in that all-too-familiar way. "What you and I think of each other is irrelevant. Annie's future and her welfare are the only things that matter."

"Have you seen the specialist?" he asked, pushing away any reference to a child he still couldn't believe was his.

"Not yet. My appointment is next week. With my primary care physician. A majority of sites on the Internet that I checked said that's the place to start. I'm seeing Rebecca Hamilton. She delivered Annie."

He hated to admit it, but that was the other reason he'd called. In spite of what she'd done—what she was trying to do—the thought of Emily being sick bothered him. But what if she was lying about the lump?

"What is it you want from me, Em?"

"*I* don't want anything."

He gripped his half full mug of cold coffee. "How do I know the baby is mine?"

"I'm more than willing to do a DNA test if that will put your mind to rest."

He didn't think there was a test in existence that would do that, not since seeing her again. "That would probably be a good idea. I'll set it up."

"Okay, then." She nodded.

"Okay."

If she was trying to pull a fast one, she wouldn't agree so easily to the test. That silenced some but not all of his doubts because being made a fool of wasn't high on his list of things to ever do again.

He'd been a teenager the last time a female had worked him over. She'd said she was pregnant and he'd believed her, married her. Months went by and she didn't show, although she jumped his bones at every opportunity. When he found out there was no baby, he knew she'd been trying to get pregnant. Her lie was exposed but he also believed her when she said she'd done it for them, so they could be together. He'd also taken it seriously when he vowed to stay together for better or worse. And worse was what he got. After that she got more creative with manipulation while their marriage died a slow and painful death. When that chapter of his life was over, he'd erased the word *commitment* from his vocabulary.

Ever since, he'd been careful about protection during sex. Because it bordered on obsession, the thought of a child had never occurred to him. That still didn't absolve Emily of fault here. She'd had a duty, an obligation, to tell him that she was going to have a baby. Too much time had passed for him to believe the child was his. She was just another woman trying to make him dance to her tune.

"So we'll wait and see what the test says," he told her.

"I have no doubt that it will confirm what I'm telling you. And I'm sorry I waited so long to do that. But I need to know she'll have her father to take care of her. If the need arises. I'm not asking for myself, but for Annie."

"So we have a plan."

"We do." She slid out of the booth. "Let me know when and where to take her for the test."

He stood and looked down at her. "Okay."

She nodded and turned away, walking between the row of booths and the swivel seats at the counter. His gaze dropped to the unconsciously sexy sway of her hips. Something tightened inside him, an ache he hadn't even been aware was there.

"Em?"

She stopped and looked back at him. "What?"

And he said something that hadn't consciously crossed his mind. "I want to see your daughter."

Chapter Two

Emily paced the living room of her ground-floor apartment waiting for Cal. Could have knocked her over with a feather when he'd called for a meeting. As angry as he was, she hadn't expected a father/daughter face-to-face until the DNA was done, so his asking to see Annie had really surprised her.

She heard an enraged wail coming from the hall and hurried to find Annie crawling—at least trying to—out of her bedroom. The little girl was in a sleeveless, white, full-skirted, lacy dress, which obviously felt like parent torture. Her knees kept getting caught up in the hem, which minimized forward progress and maximized frustration. Judging by the decibel level of the cry, her frilly frock was getting on the only nerve she had left.

Em picked up the dynamic bundle of energy. Her golden curls framed a round face with huge blue eyes and healthy, rosy cheeks.

"Hey, baby girl. I'm sorry about the dress. It's not your style, but your daddy will be here any minute and I know you want to impress him. Put your best foot forward, so to speak. Tough to do when you're not quite walking, but you get my drift. Dazzle him with your abundant charm, which you get from him, by the way."

"Unh," Annie responded, then wiggled and squirmed to be let down.

Emily complied. Carefully, she set the child on her feet, holding on to a chubby hand while Annie promptly plopped on her behind. "Putting your best foot forward needs some work, baby girl."

When she tried to crawl, her knee got tangled up in the skirt again and there was a screech that could shatter glass or set off all the dogs in the neighborhood.

Grabbing her up, Em said, "Just a little longer, sweetie. After you meet him, I'll slip you into something more comfortable. It's almost bedtime and you're not at your best, but Daddy had to work at the hospital until seven. He's a doctor, kiddo. A kiddo doctor in the emergency room. That means he only works on kids. You're gonna love him. And how could he not love you." Annie rubbed her nose on Em's shoulder leaving a slick trail of something viscous.

Em sighed at the gooey spot. "Good thing I'm not trying to impress him. You're the one he's coming to see."

She'd lost count of Annie's wardrobe changes for this auspicious occasion. Meeting your father for the first time was a big deal. Not that Em would know because she'd never laid eyes on her own dad. But surely a lady needed to look her best for something like this.

Em was well aware that she was the reason this meet and greet hadn't happened sooner and the consequences were hers to live with. But the guilt could just get in line with all the other guilts over the many mistakes she'd made. Unlike some of them, this one could be corrected. Better late than never.

The harsh sound of the bell made Em's stomach drop as if she were riding the down loop on a roller coaster. The good news was that it got Annie's attention and she stopped grunting and twisting to escape. "Here we go, sweet pea."

She carried the baby to the peephole and peeked through to establish a positive visitor ID, although Cal was right on time. When she saw him, her midsection knotted and she let out a long, bracing breath before unlocking and opening the door.

"Hi, Cal."

"Em."

She'd expected him to be in hospital scrubs, but he'd changed out of work clothes into jeans and a baby-blue shirt with actual buttons, not a T-shirt. The shade brought out the color of his eyes, his daughter's eyes. Maybe, just maybe, this meet and greet was important to him, too.

"Come in," she said, stepping back to pull the door wide before shutting it against the glare of the sun descending in the evening sky. "It's hot out there."

And in here, she thought, looking up at him. The view gave her no relief from the heat. It had been a while, but her body was still susceptible to him. Once upon a time his charm had snagged her heart, but the present vibe wasn't particularly charming so she could only assume the man himself got to her. That was too depressing to think about. And this visit wasn't about her.

Time to make long-overdue introductions.

She glanced at her daughter who was sucking on her index finger and staring uncertainly at the tall stranger. "Cal, this is Annie."

He studied her intently for a long time. Em wasn't aware of holding her breath, but let it out when he did the same.

"You didn't mention that she looks like me," he said, not taking his eyes from his daughter.

"Would you have believed me?"

"Probably not." His gaze slid to hers and turned resentful. "My hair was that color when I was little. The eyes are like mine. Even this," he said, reaching out a finger to gently touch the indentation in the little girl's chin that was identical to his own.

Annie ducked away and buried her face in Em's neck. "She's a little shy."

He nodded without saying anything and Em wished she could read his mind. Had he been hoping she'd lied? Or did the idea of having a child make him want to puff out his chest and buy a round in the pub?

"Do you want to hold her?" she asked.

"Yeah." He held out his arms and took Annie from her.

Her only intention was to make up for lost father/daughter time and she wanted it to be perfect. She should have known better. Life had been throwing her curve balls as far back as she could remember. This was no different.

Annie squirmed when he tried to settle her on his forearm. Tiny hands pushed against that wide chest and attempted to twist out of his strong grasp. Then she took one look at his face, started crying hysterically and frantically held out her hands to Em for a rescue.

"She wants you." His voice could freeze water on a Las Vegas sidewalk in July.

Em took back her baby and felt the little girl relax. Not so the unflappable E.R. doc who looked like someone had hacked his stethoscope in half. "Don't take it personally, Cal. She just needs to get to know you."

"And whose fault is it that she doesn't?"

The cutting remark hit its mark and guilt flooded her yet again. When Em felt cornered, out came the scrappy teenaged kid who'd once survived on the streets. "Look, I already admitted screwing up and apologized for it. I won't say I'm sorry again. Annie is like this with strangers, and frankly I think it's a good thing."

"It's good that she doesn't know her own father?" His eyes narrowed on her.

"Not exactly. I just meant that it's not a bad thing for her to be wary of people she doesn't know. Until she gets to know them, to separate the wheat from the chaff."

"Is that supposed to make me feel better?"

"Frankly, I can't afford to worry about how you feel." That wasn't to say she didn't worry, but it wasn't the best use of energy. "My priority is Annie."

"Mine, too, now that I know about her."

"So you really do believe she's yours? Do you still want a DNA test?"

"Yeah." He dragged his fingers through his hair. "Just to be sure."

"You don't have a lot of faith in your fellow human beings, do you?"

Before he could respond in the affirmative, the bell rang again. It startled the two adults, but also pulled Annie out of whimper mode.

"Excuse me." Em peeked out and recognized the young girl. "I have to answer this."

She opened the door and when Annie saw who was there she smiled and held out her arms.

"Hi, sugar." The green-eyed, redheaded seventeen-year-old grinned then grabbed Annie and planted kisses on both chubby cheeks, making her laugh. "How's this little girl?"

"Who wants to know?" Cal asked.

Em knew by the tone he was annoyed and had a pretty good idea why. If she'd been in his shoes it would tick her off that her child went easily to someone else and treated her like a serial killer. But that couldn't be helped.

"Cal, this is Lucy Gates. Lucy, meet Dr. Cal Westen."

The teen looked from one to the other, then at the child in her arms. "FOB?"

Cal frowned. "Friends of Bill?"

"Father of baby," Emily translated.

Nodding, he studied Lucy. "And you are?"

"One of my girls," Emily said, and knew from his skeptical expression that an explanation would be necessary. "This five-unit building was donated by Ginger Davis of The Nanny Network. With grants and donations, I run a program that mentors and houses teenage mothers. It's called Helping Hands and assists young women who have nowhere else to go. They help each other raise their babies while getting an education. Children can't be taken care of if their mothers can't take care of themselves."

Cal slid his fingertips into the pockets of his jeans. "You don't look old enough to have a baby,"

"Doesn't mean I don't," Lucy snapped back. She studied him warily. "My son's name is Oscar."

"I see."

"Right." The teen made a scoffing noise. "You don't have a clue. Just like my folks."

This wasn't going at all well, Em thought. "Lucy, he's just—"

"Judging," she snapped. "Like everyone else."

"How did your parents judge?" he asked.

Lucy's expression was a combination of hostility and hurt that she tried desperately to hide. "They threw me out when I got pregnant. Didn't want anything to do with a grandchild. Doesn't get more harsh than that."

"She and Oscar had nowhere to go," Emily explained.

The girl reminded her of herself all those years ago. When her mother gave her the ultimatum to give up her baby or get out. So, she got out. At first. But after weeks on the street, she knew she loved her child too much to subject it to that kind of life and went home, forced to make a horrible choice. Now she was trying to help young girls who were facing the same choice and give them another option.

But it was time to change the tone of this meeting. "Cal is a pediatrician," she explained to the teen.

"So you take care of kids?" Lucy asked.

"I handle pediatric emergencies at Mercy Medical Center," he said.

"So you don't do well-baby stuff? Shots and all that?"

"You need a regular pediatrician for 'stuff.'"

"So what good are you?" Lucy asked.

"If your baby has head trauma or a high fever, I'm your guy. Not so much the long-term care."

Em had never thought about it before, but even his choice of medical specialty highlighted an aversion to commitment. That didn't matter for her. Not anymore. But she wouldn't let anyone hurt her daughter. As long as Cal could commit to Annie she had no beef with him.

"Where's Oscar?" Em asked.

"With Patty."

"That's her roommate," Em explained to him. "The girls share living quarters in the apartment next door and trade off child care while working and taking classes for their GED or college credits."

"Good for them." Cal folded his arms over his chest.

Lucy sized him up, then handed Annie back to her. "I heard the dude knock on your door and wanted to make sure everything was okay."

"Thanks," Em said, taking a firm hold on the little girl who was holding out her arms again for the teenager. "It's fine. I appreciate you checking up on us."

"No problem. It's what *we* do," the teen said, giving Cal a pointed look before opening the door. "Catch you later, Em."

When they were alone again, his expression was even more hostile. "That was fun."

"She's a good kid."

"The good part I'll have to take your word on. Kid I could see for myself. My specialty is emergency care from birth to eighteen. She's young enough to be one of my patients and needs classes in birth control."

With their baby in her arms, she glared at him. "People who live in glass houses…"

"Okay." His expression turned wry. "Point taken."

"You weren't very nice to Lucy. I never knew you to be deliberately rude."

"I never had a child who treated me like I had cooties and preferred a stranger," he defended.

"Lucy isn't a stranger to Annie."

"She is to me."

"That's childish."

"But honest," he snapped.

"Unlike me."

"You said it, not me."

A guilty conscience needs no accuser. "Look, Cal, that's just the way it is. You can take it out on everyone or deal with the situation. Continue to punish me, or get to know your daughter. What's it going to be?"

"She's my child. And it's time she got to know me."

"Good."

He settled his hands on lean hips, a gunfighter's stance. "And you're going to help me."

"What does that mean?" she asked warily.

"You're going to be around while Annie and I get acquainted."

He was right. She couldn't just dump the baby on him because it would be too traumatic for them both. Emily realized that she should have seen this coming, but the truth was she hadn't. When she got the message that he'd never commit, the silver lining was not having to see him and hurt like crazy because he didn't want her the same way she'd wanted him. Ironically what broke them up was also the same thing that forced them back together.

Annie.

Emily knew what it felt like to be vulnerable and alone. Unlike FOB, she didn't plan to do that again and figured to pick and choose the people she let close to her. She'd never expected one of those people to be Cal. Again she reminded herself that he wouldn't be there for her. It was all about his child.

Gosh, wasn't it going to be fun hanging out with the guy who made breaking hearts an Olympic event?

Sitting in the sporty BMW he'd nicknamed Princess, Cal saw Emily's practical little compact come around the corner and pull into the apartment building parking area. He was across the street in front of a vacant lot and got out of his car, looking both ways to make sure there was no traffic. Ending up in his own E.R. because of stupidity would be the ultimate in humiliation, and his partners in the emergency trauma practice would show no mercy, even though he had a good excuse for being preoccupied.

As he walked toward Emily, he watched her open the rear passenger door, unbuckle Annie and lift her out. Then she went to the trunk and popped it, pulling out a plastic grocery bag. The closer he got, the more bags he could see. It never occurred to him that two girls could eat so much.

"Hi," he said.

She whirled around, clutching the child to her chest. "Good Lord, you startled me."

"I thought you saw me." He cocked a thumb over his shoulder. "I'm parked across the street."

"Why?" Her dark eyebrows drew together in a frown. "Are you stalking me?"

He slid his sunglasses to the top of his head. "Do you always go immediately to the bad place?"

"Normally, no," she said, without conviction. "But what we have here isn't a normal situation."

"What we have here probably happens more than you think," he said.

"Not in my world." She loosened her hold on Annie who was sucking on her index and middle fingers, staring at him with distrust in every cherubic curve of her face.

"Does your world still include hospital social work?"

"Yes. In addition to running Helping Hands, I freelance at most of the valley's hospitals. Not having to keep a nine-to-five schedule makes it easier to spend more time with Annie."

Occasionally a patient in the E.R. needed social services to facilitate health-care programs, hospice care or off-site treatment options. He'd met her after seeing a child with leukemia and no insurance. Em was called in to counsel the parents on available treatment and financial plans to help pay for as much as possible. He'd been anxious to turn that case over to someone else when Emily Summers had walked into the room.

One look at that face—specifically that mouth—and he'd wanted to turn himself over to her. And he had, until she'd walked out on him for no apparent reason. The fact that they were going to be parents had never entered his mind.

"So were you working today?" he casually asked. "And where does Annie stay when you can't be with her?"

"How long have you been here?"

"Not long this time."

"This time?" she asked, her eyes narrowing suspiciously.

"I stopped by earlier and talked to Lucy's roommate, Patty. She was just on her way out to a class and told me when you'd be home."

"Hmm." With a couple of grocery bags on one arm and Annie in the other, Em shifted the baby's weight.

Cal was pleased that she looked like a healthy kid. Yesterday after seeing her he realized there were a million questions he should have asked. How was the birth? Any complications? Who's her pediatrician? He could get her in with the best one in the valley.

But none of those things had come out of his mouth because he'd been too stunned that Emily told him the truth. This time he'd brought a swab and planned to get a sample for the DNA test. Skepticism had been his new best friend since the woman he'd married had lied about being pregnant so they could be together. Translation—to trap him. His first mistake was not leaving when her lie was exposed because the longer they were together, the bigger the lies got.

Last night he'd pulled out old photo albums and pored over family pictures, studying the ones of himself at Annie's age. She looked just like him. There was little doubt in his mind that she was his daughter, but because of his past, proof was required.

As he watched Emily struggle with grocery bags and the baby, it finally sank in that she could use some help. His parents hadn't raised their boys to do nothing while a woman struggled.

"Let me help you," he said, taking the bags.

"Take Annie." She thrust the little girl into his arms. "I'll grab a couple bags and unlock the door."

Instantly the child started to cry and hold out her chubby arms to her mother. Em was already hurrying to her front door, key in hand.

"Annie's crying," he called after her. "Do something."

"It's good for her lungs," she called over her shoulder. "You're a doctor. You should know that."

He *did* know that, when the child in question wasn't his and crying actual tears. "Okay, kid. Let's do this."

He grabbed as many bags as he could carry and not compromise his hold on the little girl in his arms. Fortunately Em's apartment was right around the corner from the parking lot and he followed her into the open front door. It was cool inside, a welcome relief from the July heat. The kitchen was just off the living room where Emily was half buried in the refrigerator hurriedly putting away cold and frozen food.

"What should I do with her?" he shouted over the pitiful cries that hurt his ears and his heart simultaneously.

She looked at him. "Put her on the floor."

Didn't have to tell him twice. He set Annie down on her tush where she continued to sob as if he'd been sticking pins into her.

"I'll get the rest of the bags," he said, and went to do that without waiting for permission. He was an E.R. doc and used to taking the initiative.

When he'd grabbed the remaining groceries from the trunk and shut it, he hurried back to the apartment, just as Annie was crawling out the front door. He stepped over her and dropped the bags in the middle of the living room, then raced out the door to scoop her up. The loud wail was irrefutable evidence of her displeasure. As if he needed more proof that she hated his guts.

Squirming and squealing, she continued her protest as he carried her to Em. "You've got a runner."

Em glanced over her shoulder. "Good. You got her. She tries to escape if you don't shut the door."

He put Annie on the floor and did a slow burn while Emily finished putting away the groceries. Then she grabbed up the little girl and disappeared down the hall. Cal had no choice but to follow.

He watched Em competently change the wriggling child's diaper, something he should have known to do, but didn't because he'd been left out of that particular loop. With the freshly diapered child in her arms, she went back into the kitchen and got a child's cup with a lid, filled it with water and just a splash of apple juice. He was pretty sure it was called a sippy cup because he'd heard kids in the E.R. calling them that. On the floor surrounded by plastic toys and stuffed animals, Annie grabbed the cup from her mother and chuga-lugged, evidence that she was thirsty. Or she liked her cup. Or both. He didn't know which and it ticked him off because he *should* know. He was her father.

He watched Annie put her head down on a plump stuffed bear as sucking on the juice slowed. She blinked a couple of times before her eyelids drifted closed and her hold on the cup loosened. Her breathing grew slow and even.

"She's asleep," he announced.

"I know." Em was washing apples at the sink.

"How?"

"It's late afternoon and the heat wears her out." She glanced past him and smiled tenderly. "But it's getting close to dinner time so all she gets is a power nap."

"Why?"

"If I let her sleep too long, there will be no getting her to bed at a decent hour tonight."

"Of course," he snapped.

Emily studied him. "What's bugging you?"

"Besides the fact that whenever I touch her my daughter screams as if I'm an ax murderer?"

"Yeah, besides that."

"I don't know anything about her and I'm her FOB."

"Think about it this way, Cal." Emily shut off the water, then arranged the apples along with a big bunch of green grapes in a yellow pottery bowl. "Before Annie was born I didn't know her, either. Now we've spent a little time together and I've learned about her. I do my best to make sure her needs are met so she trusts me to do that. All it takes is to put the time in. One day. Then another. And another. Until a pattern develops. If you're up for it."

"Why wouldn't I be?" he demanded.

"You're not a guy who gives patterns a chance to develop."

Not unhealthy patterns. He'd done that once and it was a disaster. "I've never had a kid before," he said, not bothering to deny her words.

"It takes time to build trust. And I get that's not easy for you, although I don't know why." She held up her hands. "You don't have to tell me. It's probably on a need-to-know basis, and I don't need to know."

She was right about that. No one needed to know that his ex gave him lesson after lesson on why women couldn't and shouldn't be trusted. Em reinforced it by keeping knowledge of his child from him. Patterns? Oh, yeah, bad ones. It's why he didn't do commitment.

"Yeah, you don't need to know," he agreed. "And you're right about spending time with her to build trust. How are we going to work that out?"

"I'm not sure yet. But we will."

Looking around the apartment, he assessed his daughter's environment. He recognized the light green corner group from Em's other place and the cherrywood coffee table in front of it. There was a TV on a stand in the corner that was also familiar. Three wrought-iron barstools with beige seats lined up at the counter separating the kitchen and living room. They were new because her old place hadn't had a bar. If he walked in her bedroom, would the floral comforter be there? More than once he'd swept it to the floor in his hurry to have her.

His body tightened and he remembered that, too, the intensity of his need for her. It was different from the way he'd wanted any other woman. And he still felt it, which didn't make him at all happy.

"Do you need money?" he asked.

"No." The indignation in her expression was easy to read.

"I don't mean to offend you, but I have nine months of pregnancy, the birth and eleven months of Annie's life that I owe you for."

"You don't owe me anything," she said, anger flashing briefly in her eyes "Money isn't why I told you about her. I just wanted you to know she exists. In case anything happens to me."

The lump in her breast. He'd forgotten that what with the mess of finding out he was a father. She'd said she had an appointment.

"I'll go with you to see the doctor." If she was lying about it this would call her bluff.

"I can handle it."

"I'm not saying you can't." He ran his fingers through his hair. "Just that you might need some help with Annie."

"That's not a problem," she protested. "I'm used to taking her with me."

"No offense, but she's got a pretty good set of lungs. That could make actually hearing what the doc has to say difficult."

"I can leave her with Lucy—"

"No." Anger knotted in his gut. "Annie is my daughter. I can stay in the waiting room with her. Just a short-term assignment."

"Are you sure?" Em caught the corner of her bottom lip between her teeth.

"Absolutely." And he absolutely couldn't look away from those small, straight white teeth sinking into the soft flesh of her mouth. It made him think about the rest of her flesh—the parts underneath her clothes. That made him want to get her naked, which was a very big problem.

"Okay, then," she agreed. "You can come with me."

"Good. It will go a long way toward establishing trust."

With his daughter, not with Emily. She'd burned him once and wouldn't get another chance. After doing the deceit dance with his ex-wife, he knew that second chances were a slow slide to the dark side. Lori always had an ulterior motive for the suicide attempts that never succeeded. It kept him with her, at least until the next time he got fed up and threatened to leave when she'd try again and wind up in the E.R. to make a dramatic statement. Then, without warning, she'd left him first. Where was the win in that?

And Emily had done the same thing. But now she was back. That just meant this was a new challenge, that there was something she wanted more than getting him together with his daughter.

All he had to do was find out what that something was and beat her at her own game.

Chapter Three

As she walked through the medical building's courtyard, Emily carried Annie. Cal was beside them, hefting the diaper bag. Part of her couldn't help thinking of him as her knight in shining armor. The street-smart side knew there was no such thing.

He'd offered her money, for Pete's sake. Like he thought she wanted something besides security for their daughter if the breast lump turned out to be cancer. Playing the money card was like waving the red penalty flag saying he didn't trust her. As if she needed more proof, he'd swabbed Annie's mouth for the DNA sample. He'd looked like he felt bad about making her cry, but their little girl, just like her mother, showed no signs of forgiving or forgetting and wanted nothing to do with him today.

Her appointment was for nine o'clock and they were ten minutes early. The shady courtyard was cool this time of day, relatively speaking since it was July. Desert landscaping dominated the center with rocks and plants in shades of purple, yellow, orange and pink.

Emily stopped and pointed to the last door on the right. "Here's the office."

"Okay."

"There's no guarantee that I'll be taken in right on time."

"I'm a doctor. I get it," Cal said wryly.

"You work in the E.R. Rebecca Hamilton is a busy ob-gyn. That's like comparing apples and kumquats." She shifted Annie in her arms. "There's a fifty-fifty chance that we're going to have to wait. Her appointments always get juggled because of deliveries. Babies have a complete disregard for schedules and office hours. They arrive on their own time regardless of who it inconveniences."

"What time was Annie born?" he asked quietly. Black-framed sunglasses hid his eyes and their expression, which was probably just as well.

Em rubbed a hand down her daughter's back. "A respectable seven o'clock in the morning."

"Good for her." He started to walk past her. "Okay. I get it. We'll probably have to wait."

"Hold it. You might want some helpful hints."

"Such as?"

"All indications are that Annie's going to have some serious misgivings when I give her to you. Your assignment, if you choose to accept it, is to keep her safe and as happy as possible." She tightened her hold on the little girl in her arms. "If she tries to get down, put her down. Let her do what she wants as long as she doesn't bother anyone or hurt herself. Try to distract her with a toy. I packed her favorites, a sippy cup and crackers. Don't worry about the mess in the waiting room."

"Mess?"

"You'll find out."

He nodded. "Got it."

"Can you change a diaper?"

"Did you pack a schematic?"

"Very funny." She couldn't help smiling. His sense of humor was the first thing that attracted her. Now was no exception. "A simple yes or no will suffice."

"I think I can figure it out."

"If nothing makes her happy and she won't stop crying, remove her from the waiting room. She loves being outside and hopefully that will distract her. If not, go to the reception desk and Grace will come to the exam room and get me."

"Grace?"

"Martinson. She's the doctor's receptionist, office manager and all around assistant."

"Got it." He shifted the strap of the diaper bag more securely on his broad shoulder.

Emily knew for a fact that the thing was heavy yet he didn't seem to feel the weight. But Annie's bulk was starting to make her back hurt. If only she could pass the child to Cal, but that would start a meltdown, not a smart move until it was absolutely necessary.

"Okay." She took a deep breath and started down the cement pathway toward the office. "Let's do this."

"This" was the last thing she wanted to do, but the lump hadn't gone away. Inside, the waiting room was air-conditioned and there was only one woman waiting, meaning either the doctor was on time or there'd been a delivery and earlier patients rescheduled. Either way it was a good thing for them.

Emily signed the patient sheet with her name and arrival time, then found a bench seat by the back office door. She settled Annie on her lap and Cal sat beside her.

The older woman in the chair next to them smiled. "Your little girl is adorable."

Although she didn't feel like small talk, Em could never ignore an Annie compliment. "Thank you. I think so, too."

"She looks just like her daddy," the woman said.

Cal nodded. "I think so, too."

"How old is she?"

He looked at Em who answered, "Almost a year."

The woman nodded. "You make a lovely family."

If they were giving off a family vibe, it was Academy Award–caliber performances. This was the first outing for the three of them, and not for happy reasons. Fortunately no response was required because the door opened and Grace Martinson stood there. Emily had gotten to know her pretty well during her prenatal visits.

The green-eyed redhead in blue scrubs smiled. "Hi, Em. I'll take you back in a minute. Mrs. Wilson?"

The older woman stood and followed her into the back office. Em's stomach did the nervous dance with a healthy dose of fear driving it. All her research said that 80 percent of breast lumps turned out to be benign, but what if she was in the 20 percent range? She squeezed Annie to her until the little girl squirmed in protest. What would happen to this child if something happened to her? Her own mother wouldn't win any awards, but at least she'd been around. Sort of.

She glanced at Cal who'd slid his sunglasses to the top of his head and looked ultra-cool and devastatingly handsome. He'd have to take care of their child on his own. In a few minutes he was going to get a crash course demonstrating exactly what that meant. Before she could give him last-minute pointers, the door opened again and Grace was there.

"You're up, Emily."

"Okay." She stood with Annie in her arms and kissed her daughter's cheek. Then she looked at Cal. "You're up, too."

He nodded and held out his arms. She handed the baby

over and steeled herself for the cry of protest that came instantly.

"I'll get her back as quick as I can," Grace said to him, then shut the door.

Em followed her to the first exam room where she was directed to disrobe from the waist up and put on a cloth gown. Left alone, she did as instructed, all the while hoping her baby's cries would diminish and stop, but no such luck. She heard the front door open and close. He was following orders and taking Annie outside, which meant juice and favorite crackers had no effect on her daughter's aversion to the complete stranger who was her father.

Em felt like the worst mother on the planet, and the slime at the bottom of a toxic pond. This was all her fault. It wouldn't be this traumatic if Annie knew Cal and that was something she'd regret to her dying day, which hopefully wouldn't be too soon.

It made her angry that she was faced with a situation she couldn't control and had to rely on Cal. Even more, she hated how glad she was that he was there, but none of this was fair to Annie. She had no idea what was going on and was just scared because her mommy had thrust her into the arms of a man she didn't know from a rock. No wonder she was crying her eyes out. That, at least, was something that could be fixed.

She opened the door to the exam room, held her gown together with one hand at her chest and flagged Grace down in the hallway. "Annie's really upset."

"I heard," Grace said ruefully.

"Can she come in the exam room?"

"It will be hard for the doctor to check you out if she's clinging to you."

"As long as she can see me, I think it would calm her down," Em said.

"Who's the hunk?" Grace asked.

"Dr. Cal Westen."

"The pediatric E.R. guy at Mercy Medical? He's a friend?"

Not so much, Em thought. "You could say that."

Grace looked puzzled. "What about patient privacy?"

"I want him to know everything. Just in case."

"Okay." Grace nodded. "I'll go get him."

Em nodded then sat on the exam table, legs dangling over the end. Moments later she heard Annie crying and it got louder just before Cal brought her into the room.

He handed the baby to her. "Sorry."

That made two of them. "Not your fault," she said, cuddling the little girl to her. "Can I have her cup?"

He dug the juice out of the diaper bag and Annie grabbed it, relaxing in her arms when she started to suck.

"Do you want me to leave?" he asked.

"No." She didn't want to be alone, and Annie didn't count.

The crying jag had worn her out and a bit of gentle rocking coaxed her into sleep. "Can you take her? It will be fine. Once she goes off, it takes a lot to wake her."

He nodded and set the diaper bag on the chair, then stood in front of her and held out his arms. True to form, Annie slept through the transfer and Em's arms were grateful. Moments later the doctor walked in. A brown-eyed blonde, Rebecca Hamilton was in her late twenties, young for a doctor. She'd skipped several grades in school and that had given her a jump on her career and a successful, growing practice.

"Hi, Emily," she said, settling her wire-rimmed glasses more securely on her freckle-splashed nose. She noticed Cal and the baby. "Sorry. I didn't know Annie was asleep."

"This is Cal Westen," Emily said. "He's a doctor."

Rebecca nodded. "I know you by reputation, Doctor, and I mean that in a good way."

"Same here," he said.

Rebecca looked at her. "So you brought along moral support?"

Em nodded. "Kind of. He's Annie's father."

"I see." There was no indication that Rebecca was surprised, but then she'd probably heard it all. "So, let's get down to business."

She did the usual listen with the stethoscope and took a pulse and blood pressure. Then she stood between Emily and Cal as she parted the gown and did an exam of the left breast. Frowning, she said, "There it is."

Em was hoping this had all been her imagination and took a deep breath. "Is it cancer?"

"Don't go there," Rebecca advised. "We have absolutely no reason to believe that. More information is required to determine exactly what it is. Could be a cyst, which is no big deal. Or a noncancerous mass such as a fibroadenoma, a benign tumor. Or an intraductal papilloma."

"Translation?" Em said, pulling the gown closed over her breasts.

"That's a small, wartlike growth in a milk duct. Since you nursed Annie, that would be my guess. But we need to do some tests."

"Mammogram?" Cal asked.

Rebecca glanced over her shoulder, then looked back at Em. "Because you're so young, I'd like to start with an ultrasound. It's noninvasive, painless and radiation free. It should determine if the lump is a mass or just a harmless, fluid-filled cyst. If that's the case, testing is over and there's nothing to fear. Although we might want to aspirate the contents."

"What if it's not?" Cal asked.

"Then we get a diagnostic mammogram. It's a digital, electronic image," she explained to Em, because he already knew this stuff. "The pictures can be computer manipulated, making them cleaner, clearer and easier to read. We focus on the area of concern, compressing tissue and magnifying images so that we can get a much more detailed look."

"Will that tell us what it is?" Em asked.

"We'll know more about what it isn't," Rebecca explained. "If it's not a cyst, we'll need a biopsy."

"Surgery?" Em's heart started to hammer and she met Cal's eyes over the doctor's shoulder.

"No." Rebecca touched her hand. "An ultrasound-guided core needle biopsy. It's an in-office procedure to extract a small sampling of cells, which we'll test. I want to stress that there's absolutely no reason for you to believe the worst. If you'd like, I can recommend a breast specialist. Or I'd be happy to consult with one and coordinate your care."

Emily glanced at Cal, still holding a peacefully sleeping Annie. Emotion swelled inside her and pressed against her heart. "What do you think?"

"Dr. Hamilton is right. It's one step at a time. If you're comfortable, it's clear that she's got the situation under control."

"Here is good."

The doctor nodded. "Then for now I'll coordinate everything. I'm going to have Grace set up an appointment at the breast imaging center at Mercy Medical. That's step one. And you're not to worry."

"Right."

Rebecca put a reassuring arm around her shoulders and said, "It's going to be okay."

When they were alone, Cal let out a breath. He looked like he'd worked a double shift in the E.R. during cold and flu season. "How are you?"

"Probably better than you."

He glanced at the little girl cradled in his arms. "It's been a rough morning."

"There's the understatement of the century." She met his gaze. "I want to go home."

He nodded. "I'll take her in the waiting room so you can get dressed."

"Thanks, Cal."

And she didn't mean for leaving her alone. He'd hung in there with Annie. And with her. Running interference with the medical stuff. Advice. A sounding board. She could have done it on her own, but she was incredibly glad that hadn't been necessary. Far too glad.

Too glad meant she had lingering feelings rattling around inside her. When she'd made the decision to tell him about his daughter, she'd been so sure that wasn't possible. Now she knew she was wrong. Leftover feelings were like embers after a forest fire, which could burst into flame with very little encouragement.

Considering he didn't trust her as far as he could throw her, that made it a one-way street. Just like the last time and the scars on her heart were a continuing reminder of how that had turned out.

Cal now knew that Emily wasn't lying, at least not about the lump in her breast. He'd thought about little else since leaving the doctor's office yesterday and still didn't know what to think or how to feel. That was the only reason he could come up with for stopping by her apartment without calling.

After parking across the street, he knocked on Em's door and waited. When there was no answer, he tried again and the door beside hers opened.

Redheaded Lucy Gates stood there and somewhere behind her there was a child crying. "What do you want?"

Great. Miss Congeniality. "I stopped by to see Emily. And Annie."

"Em's not home." Distrust rolled off her in waves.

"I see. Do you have any idea when she'll be back?"

She glanced over her shoulder and called out, "Patty? Did Em say how long she'll be?" The answer was muffled and she said, "Soon."

"Patty. Your roommate."

"Right." Her hostile look didn't change, so it was a good guess that there were no points for remembering that. The child was still making unhappy noises.

"Who's crying?" he asked.

Lucy's expression asked why he cared, but she answered, "Henry."

"Who's Henry?"

"Patty's little boy. He's sick," she volunteered.

"What's wrong with him?"

She shrugged. "Probably a cold."

"Fever?" he asked.

"Yeah. A little bit."

"Do you want me to take a look at him?" Cal asked.

"I thought you didn't do that stuff. It's not an emergency—" She glanced over her shoulder when someone behind her spoke. "You're a doctor, right? A pediatrician?"

"That's what my diploma says. Does Henry have a pediatrician?"

"Not a regular one. We take the kids to a clinic." Again, there was a muffled voice before she opened the door wider. "But maybe it wouldn't hurt for you to have a look at him."

Cal nodded and stepped inside on the beige carpet. From what he could see, this apartment was a carbon copy of Emily's floor plan—living room, small kitchen with dinette and a hall with two bedrooms on each side of it. On one wall sat a re-covered sofa, not a professional job, but still a charming floral print. The coffee table looked like a do-it-yourself dark-stained plywood number, but complemented the rest of the decor. The walls were filled with photos of children and kid-friendly prints. Other than toys scattered around, the place was spotless.

A blond girl about Lucy's age stepped forward with a whimpering, sniffling, towheaded toddler in her arms. "I'm Patty. And this is Henry."

"Hi."

"Lucy said you're a doctor."

"That's right."

"Since you're here… Would it be okay for you to take a quick look at him?" she asked, worry widening her big blue eyes. She should be at cheerleader practice and fretting about finals, not sharing an apartment with another teen mother.

"Sure."

Another baby, Oscar, he remembered, was on a quilt beside the sofa with stuffed animals spread out around him. The little guy looked clean and well fed, what with the chubby arms and legs sticking out of his denim overalls.

Cal walked over and said to the under-the-weather boy in her arms, "Hey, buddy. You're not feeling so good?"

The kid's nasal discharge was clear, a positive indicator of no infection. Cal palpated his neck for enlarged lymph nodes or swelling and didn't find anything abnormal. "He feels warm."

"I just took his temp," Patty said. "It's a hundred."

Cal nodded. "That's not too bad. Do you have a flashlight?"

Lucy looked more puzzled than hostile now. "What for?"

"I'd like to look in his throat and I can see what's going on better with a light."

"We have one in the kitchen," Patty said, walking into the room and opening a drawer.

"Set him on the counter for me, and let's see if we can get him to open wide," he directed. "How old is he?"

"Eighteen months."

Patty did as directed and when Cal came close, Henry started to cry, which meant opening his mouth. *Attaboy.* He aimed the light and saw some mild redness, which was probably a result of postnasal drip. "I don't have an otoscope—"

"A what?" Lucy asked.

"That's the thing the doctor at the clinic uses to check their ears," Patty answered.

"Right," Cal said. "Has he been pulling at them?"

"No." Patty held on to Henry's arm with one hand and smoothed the hair off his forehead with the other. "He had one ear infection when he was six months old and I've been watching for that. But he's just not acting like himself."

Cal didn't have a stethoscope on him, either, so he pressed his ear to the boy's chest and back, listening for any evidence of wheezing or labored breathing but breath sounds were normal.

Patty grabbed the whimpering child when he held out his arms to her. "Is he okay?"

"I think it's just a cold."

"That's what I said," Lucy reminded him.

"Is there some medicine he should take?" Patty asked, shooting her roommate a stand-down stare.

"A children's fever reducer will make him more comfortable. At this point an antibiotic won't help because as far as I can tell it's nothing more than a virus." Which Henry had probably already shared with his pint-size roommate. "Is Oscar showing signs of not feeling well?"

"Not yet," Lucy said. "But I'm watching him. We're trying to keep the kids separated as much as possible."

"That would be best. And be sure to wash your hands often." Cal nodded. "As far as any other medications, they're not indicated yet. If he takes unnecessary antibiotics, he'll build up a tolerance and they won't work when he really needs them."

"Okay." Patty nodded. "Is there anything else I should do?"

"Push fluids. Diluted soda. Juice. Popsicles. Water. Make sure his diapers are wet. That means he's good and hydrated."

"I've been doing that," Patty told him.

"And if his fever goes up to a hundred and two, bring him to see me in the E.R. at Mercy Medical Center."

"As if," Lucy said.

"What?" he asked.

"We can't afford to go there," Patty explained, looking apologetic. "No medical insurance. If either of them needs to go to the E.R. I'm not sure what we'd do."

"Emily will know," Lucy said. "She always finds a way."

"I don't know what we'd do without her," Patty agreed.

Both girls spoke about Emily Summers as if she had wings, a halo and walked on water. But he knew better. Angels didn't lie about having a guy's baby. Just because she'd told the truth about the lump didn't mean he could forget about the months of his daughter's life that she'd stolen from him.

There was a knock on the door and Lucy went to answer it. "Hi, Em."

"Hey. How's Henry?"

"The doc says it's probably just a cold," the teen explained.

"The doc?" Emily took one step inside holding Annie in her arms. "Cal?"

"Hi." He watched Annie babble something and squirm to get down, but her mom held her tight. That was a good thing since she shouldn't get too close to Henry.

"What are you doing here?" she asked him.

"I was in the neighborhood," he hedged.

"Right." Her tone clearly indicated she didn't buy that for a second. Without moving any farther inside, she handed a small, white bag to Lucy. "I got the children's' Tylenol for you."

"Thanks."

"I hope Henry feels better soon," she said, sending a sympathetic glance in his direction.

"Me, too." Patty handed him a sippy cup and he started drinking.

"I need to get this little girl home," Emily said, backing out of the apartment.

Cal followed her, then looked back at the teens. "If you have any questions…"

"Thanks, Doctor," Patty said. "I really appreciate you looking at him."

"You're welcome."

He followed Emily into her apartment next door. As she bent over to pick up a toy, his attention was drawn to her shapely body. In her sleeveless, white-cotton sundress and matching low-heeled sandals, she looked like an angel. Although there was just enough wickedness in her wind-blown dark hair to speed up his heart. The wispy silky strands around her face reminded him of all the times he'd run his hands through it while loving her. Something tightened low and deep in his gut, and his hands ached to pull her against him, just like old times. Then he got a good look at the expression on her face.

"What are you doing here?" she asked again. "And we both know this neighborhood isn't your usual stomping grounds."

"I stopped by to see Annie." *Mostly.*

She set their daughter on the floor. "It would have been nice if you'd called first."

It would have if he'd actually planned ahead for this. "I'll keep that in mind."

As if registering her protest was enough, the indignation seemed to drain out of her. "Thanks for taking a look at Henry."

"No problem."

"The girls are barely getting by on welfare, food stamps

and small subsidies from a children's foundation. Without Helping Hands, they'd probably be in a women's shelter. If they were lucky. The street is the only other option." A dark look slid into her eyes. "So you can see that private medical insurance isn't in the budget."

"They told me."

"And there's not enough money to pay for an office visit."

"Where are the kids' fathers?" Cal asked.

"Lucy hasn't seen Oscar's dad since telling him about the pregnancy. Her parents kicked her out when she broke the news to them." The disapproval on her face and contempt in her voice said loud and clear what she thought about that. "Henry's dad, Jonas Blackford, is making minimum wage working for one of the local hotels and he's taking college classes. An education is the only way to get ahead and make a better life for his son. Financially he does what he can and stops by to see the boy every day. They're not married, but doing their best to raise Henry together. You have to respect that."

Did he? When you made a mistake, you tried to do the right thing. That's the way his parents had raised him. Annie was watching him while she chewed on the yellow plastic key that was hooked to a red, blue and green one. She took it out of her mouth and banged it several times, blinking as if she'd surprised herself. Then she threw them down and crawled over to where he and Em were talking, the first time she'd voluntarily come this close to him. Although from what he'd seen she had no problem with the teens next door. The baby put a hand on her mother's dress and pulled herself to a standing position while staring up at him.

"So," he said, "Annie seems pretty comfortable with Lucy."

"Patty, too. She's over there all the time. They watch her for me if I have to run to the store, or I get an unexpected call to work and haven't lined up child care."

"I could help with that."

"You have to work, too," she pointed out. "But I appreciate the offer."

He smiled at Annie who was blinking up at him and out of the blue, she returned his smile. A big, warm feeling swelled inside him, followed by a free fall into never-ending tenderness. And a sensation of wanting to keep her safe from anything and everything that could hurt her.

"You know Henry's probably contagious," he said.

"Poor baby." She sighed. "Yeah, I know."

"Annie should keep her distance."

"Of course. But it's hard." She reached a hand down to steady the little girl, then eased her to a sitting position. "She loves those little boys. The three of them are like siblings."

And like a lot of what was going on lately he wasn't sure how he felt about that. An instant later words came out of his mouth before he could think them through or stop them.

"You and Annie should move in with me."

Chapter Four

Emily stared at Cal for several moments. "I must be more tired than I realized. You'll never guess what I thought you just said."

"You heard right. It's a good idea for you and Annie to move into my house."

Once upon a time she'd have given anything to hear those words, but now they just gave her a bad feeling. "Why?"

"I know what you're thinking."

"Which is?" she asked.

He looked down at their daughter, clinging to her skirt. "That this is just because of Annie."

"That's not even close," she told him. "But now that you mention it..."

"It's a big house."

She picked Annie up and balanced her on a hip, then went to the kitchen to get her some water. After settling her on the floor with an assortment of toys, she moved closer to Cal and looked up.

"I remember exactly how big your place is. I've been there. Maybe you forgot."

"Hardly." Heat flashed through his eyes for just a moment, a sign that he hadn't forgotten the way they'd burned up the sheets. "But you told me once that it's a pretty big place for one person."

She remembered. That was during her brain-hiccup phase when she thought they might have had a chance at happiness. "I stand by that."

"And I agree with you." He grinned the grin that brought women to their knees. "It's also in a great neighborhood."

Emily's knees threatened, but she refused to buckle. Especially when she understood the subtext of his remark—by comparison to his big house and great neighborhood where she lived was lacking. She folded her arms over her chest. "I don't think it's paranoia leaping to the conclusion that you think Annie's current neighborhood isn't up to Spanish Trail's standards."

"That's not what I meant."

"Then let me put a finer point on your meaning. You don't want Annie hanging out with anyone who doesn't meet your personal standards." A long time ago when she'd been impossibly young and pregnant, she'd been the girl no parent wanted their daughter to hang out with. Part of that lonely, humiliated girl still lived inside her.

"I meant that it would be easier to control her surroundings. When you go to work or the store, she wouldn't have to stay in a germ-filled environment."

"Oh, please. The world is full of germs. There's no way to protect her from that, Cal. You're a doctor. Isn't that taught in Microbiology 101, or something?"

"Or something." He rubbed a hand across the back of his neck. "But right now she's unnecessarily exposed to stuff. For your information, that's a professional opinion. As you pointed out, I am a doctor."

She really wanted to be bitchy and mad at him, but two things stopped her. Dressed in a black T-shirt tucked into worn jeans gave him serious points for cute. And thing number two had a lot to do with how darned endearing he was being in trying to protect his child. He had great instincts. With a little training, he'd be an outstanding dad who'd take really good care of their child, if the need should arise.

And if she could be personally objective, his invitation would merit some thought. But she'd never been able to be impartial about Cal Westen. He was an all-or-nothing-at-all kind of guy.

"I'm running the Helping Hands program. I mentor the teens and part of my responsibility is being accessible to them."

"You couldn't be accessible from my place?"

"Even if I wanted to, you live on the other side of town. If Lucy or Patty, or the boys need me, I'd be too far away."

"Isn't Annie more important?" Feet planted wide apart, he rested his hands on lean hips and glanced at the baby, happily babbling while playing with a stuffed doll.

"She's the most important person in the world. And I'd never do anything to compromise her welfare." She took a deep breath. "But those teenagers and the children they've brought into the world are important, too. They need guidance more than ever because of the little boys depending on them. And because their families threw them away when they got pregnant they have no support system and nowhere to go."

She didn't miss his small wince and knew he was remembering his soliloquy on the benefits of being alone. "To remain here, they must go to school, either for a GED, college classes or a vocational program. I insist on it because the only way they'll be able to take care of themselves and their kids is with an education. With help, they can raise their children *and* become productive members of society, instead of living dependent, wasted lives."

Emily hadn't had the choice to keep her baby. She'd loved her child with every fiber of her being and couldn't bear the thought of him being hungry, cold or sick. She couldn't bear it if he'd needed something she couldn't give him because she was too selfish to do the right thing. Her baby boy had needed a warm place to live with a father and mother who wanted him more than anything.

Cal blew out a long breath. "You're really dedicated to these kids, aren't you?"

"Absolutely," she answered without hesitation.

"Why?"

Her reasons were deeply personal. Though giving him up for adoption was the right thing, it still pained her unbearably when she wondered if he was doing okay. Did he ever think she hadn't cared about him? Was he angry and resentful that he didn't know his biological mother? Did he have any idea what he'd have endured if she hadn't made the choice to give him away?

Her motivation was to save as many girls as possible from having to go through a similar agonizing experience. But all she said was, "It's the right thing to do."

"I know all about doing the right thing," he said.

"Of course you do. You're the guy in the white hat. The knight in shining armor."

"When I was in medical school the time came when I had to decide on a specialty—medical or surgical. And I picked emergency medicine for children."

"Because you like the adrenaline rush of the emergency room," she guessed.

"It's more than that. The kids I see usually have parents who are emotionally invested in their children. They'd move heaven and earth to make them better. Do what it takes for a good outcome. And I never see those kids again."

"Which is the goal," she said.

"Right." He ran his fingers through his hair. "But they're the kind of moms and dads who'd pick up and move if there was a better place to raise an asthmatic child. Mortgage their life to the hilt to pay for whatever treatment necessary to make a child well."

They'd talked about this once. She knew he was dedicated to saving every child in the E.R. whose life was at risk and would never understand that she'd given her child up for the very same reason.

"Your goal is to never see a child in your E.R. again. My girls need ongoing help and I won't abandon them."

"Even if Annie would be better off somewhere else?"

"Look, Cal, do you really think I'm a bad mother? Because a bad mother wouldn't put her child first and—"

"That's not what I'm saying—"

"Yes, you are." She put her hands on her hips as she stared up at him. "Everything I do, every decision I make is with Annie's welfare in mind. Including telling you that you have a child in case something happens to me. And right now I have to say that's a decision I'm beginning to regret."

"And why is that?"

"You're butting into my life," she answered.

"Did you really think you could tell me about my child and not expect me to become involved?"

"You wouldn't be the first," she said, thinking about the first biological father she'd never set eyes on. And *she'd* never felt as alone as that fifteen-year-old girl who told the boy she'd slept with that he was going to be a father, then never seen him again.

"I'm not like Lucy's FOB."

"I agree. Complete opposite. You drop by unannounced." What she didn't share was how happy she'd been to see him, which was part of the reason she was on the defensive now.

"If I'd called, would you have made an excuse to put me off?" he asked. "Or keep me from coming over because there was something you didn't want me to see?"

"I get it. Really." Em pointed at him. "You don't trust me. You didn't believe I was telling the truth about Annie being yours or that I have a lump."

"Can you blame me?"

No, but he'd never hear that from her. "I'm not going to live my life proving that everything I say or do is sincere and truthful. I don't lie, Cal."

"Except by omission."

"I'm not perfect. I make mistakes but apparently the people in your world aren't allowed that luxury."

"That's a little harsh."

"Then why did you go into guard-duty-surveillance mode?" she demanded.

"I think that's a father's prerogative," he retorted. "Just like you're doing with Helping Hands."

"I won't let those girls be alone." Not like she'd been.

"And I won't let Annie be alone. Wasn't that why you came to me in the first place?"

"Yes," she admitted.

"Then you can't have it both ways. You can't tell me she exists then keep me out of the loop. I'm not irresponsible. I'll step up and take care of her, but I want a say in what happens. Legal rights."

"Okay."

He blinked. "As easy as that?"

"You call this easy?"

"Now that you mention it…"

Annie crawled over and pulled herself to a standing position, again using Em's skirt for leverage. She picked her up and settled her on a hip. "Hey, baby girl."

Em had never thought of herself as the kind of woman who didn't share well, but now she wondered if Cal was right about her wanting it both ways. She'd worked very hard for her independence because she never wanted to need anyone again. Then she'd met Cal and made the mistake of letting him in once.

It was obvious that her attraction hadn't ended with their relationship, which meant stopping it altogether would be about as easy as reversing the effects of global warming. She'd tried to forget him, but never quite managed to pull that off. Maybe because he'd fathered her baby.

The fact was they were both responsible for this child and he was determined to be a father, so she needed to find a path to peaceful coexistence. But moving in with him, relying on him, leaning on him was a path she wouldn't go down.

He smiled at Annie, who looked more curious than wary. "Is that a truce?"

"I think a cease fire is an excellent idea," Em agreed.

And she hoped she didn't regret those words. It would be so easy to fall in love with him and that scared her more than being alone.

Cal wasn't above bribery. His goal was to know his daughter and if that meant buying Annie's good will so be it. He wanted Em's as well, which was why he'd called first before showing up at her door bearing gifts galore for his child. All age appropriate, of course.

He rang the bell, not easy with his arms full. Since seeing over the stack was difficult, it was more by sound that he knew when Em answered the door. And laughed. God, he'd always loved her laugh, a sound so full of amusement it always made him smile.

"Cal? Is that you? Or did Santa and the elves make a major screw up?"

"Ho, ho, ho."

She laughed again, but he wouldn't let it make him smile. A truce only meant he had to get along with her. Nothing in the rules said he had to like her. No way was he getting sucked in again by a deceitful woman. He'd married the first one and divorce ended any obligation to communicate. He'd fathered a child with the second and communication was required if he wanted to know his daughter. But as far as his attraction to untrustworthy women was concerned, it was way past time to break that pattern. And he was trying his best to ignore how much he was still attracted to this one.

"Come on in, St. Nick."

Her sweetly seductive voice conjured up visions a saint wouldn't know anything about, proving that Cal was no saint. He remembered her throaty moans when he kissed her breasts and belly and a sensitive spot behind her knee. The memory made him hot all over, a heat that had nothing to do with triple-digit temps in the Vegas Valley.

He set the stack of boxed toys down just inside the door. In the center of the living room, Annie's big blue eyes followed his every move. With interest instead of wariness, he noted. That was a step in the right direction. Her blond hair was still damp, evidence that her mom had already bathed her before bedtime. The little girl wore pink princess pajamas with a tank top and shorts bottoms. It was all he could do to keep from grabbing her up and hugging her tight.

And that's what ticked him off the most. He knew how to

eal with kids of all ages who came to see him in the E.R. This
ttle girl was his flesh and blood, and he didn't have a clue how
) proceed. Except that he didn't want to make her cry again.

He looked at Em who was also watching him. She was
earing a yellow camisole-type tank with white shorts that
evealed her smooth, tanned legs. His palms itched to slide
ver that soft flesh and make her quiver with desire the way
he once had. A lifetime ago. A time before he knew what she
as capable of. It was on the tip of his tongue to lash out,
ecause anger made a great shield against the strong feelings
e couldn't control. If there were a surgical alternative, he'd
ladly go under the knife. For now all he could do was pray
or winter when she'd need to wear more clothes.

"So," he said, selecting a package on the top of the stack.
le walked past Annie whose gaze followed him all the way
) the sofa where he sat. "I picked up a few things."

"Yes, you did. If this is for nothing, I can only imagine what
er first birthday will be like in a couple weeks."

At least he hadn't missed out on that milestone. "I didn't
acrifice quality for quantity. Everything here meets the age
:iteria. Not a choking hazard in the bunch."

"I'd expect nothing less of Mercy Medical's pediatric
.R. star."

"Star?" He shrugged. "I wouldn't go that far."

"Apparently that's not your call to make. The *Review
ournal* has none of your self-deprecating modesty." She
)inted to the Las Vegas newspaper on the bar. "They did an
xtensive article about the hospital's emergency room staffing
 pediatric trauma specialist 24/7."

"Yeah. Administration has been pushing the idea for a long
me. Jake, Mitch and I need to find a couple of pediatric
auma specialists for the group so we can increase our E.R.
)verage. I remember talking to a reporter about it a few

weeks ago." He put the toy on her coffee table. "I didn't thin
they were going to use the material."

Em put her hands on shapely hips, a pose that did amazin
things to her already amazing body. "Think again. Ther
were pictures."

"Oh?"

She nodded. "Of you. In action. But the text included lot
of nurse comments about the playboy, bachelor doctor who'
so good with the littlest patients. I believe the last part of th
article said something like, 'He's dated half the women in th
Vegas Valley and after reading this the other half will b
forming a line for introductions.'"

He didn't deny it. There was a reason every TV soap oper
featured a hospital. Rumors and stories spread faster than a
immunization-resistant strain of the flu. The truth was, h
dated. A lot. But as soon as a woman made noises about takin
things to the next level he put on the brakes so no one got hur

Cal studied her, trying to figure out if his active social lif
bothered her, but her expression gave no hint. It wouldn'
bother him one bit if she *was* bothered. As the saying went–
payback was hell.

While he and Em talked, Annie crawled over to the stac
of toys piled by the door and used it as leverage to stand
Babbling like crazy, she smacked her little hand on the cello
phane covering of a play set that included a Cinderella coac
and fairy-tale figures. With a sweeping motion, she pushe
that aside and did the same thing to the toddler radio jus
underneath it.

Emily squatted down beside her. "Be nice, Annie. You
daddy brought these for you. Can you say thank you to Daddy?

Daddy? The single word filled him with awe as well as th
awesome responsibility the title implied. Protection. Gu
dance. Welfare. Education. And a lot of other components tha

made up childhood and would shape his little girl into a productive woman. Which is what Em was doing with her Helping Hands program. Respect for her efforts threatened, but he wasn't going there.

"I wanted to get her a fancy doll, but there were multiple warning labels." He smiled at Annie who'd stopped babbling when she heard his voice. "Have you ever noticed that three is the magic age where the toy world opens wide?"

"As a matter of fact I have noticed," Em agreed. Her dark eyes sparkled with humor. "I'm guessing that's the magic age when she'll stop putting everything in her mouth, which cancels out the choking hazard."

He nodded. "Then we have to hope she doesn't put stuff in her nose and ears instead."

"Oh, God," Em groaned. "You're kidding, right?"

He shook his head. "It's not the number one trauma, but you wouldn't believe what I've had to extract."

She steadied Annie and slid him a look somewhere between wry and concerned. "The world of toys and toddlers is a very scary place for a parent."

"Tell me about it."

Was this parental bonding? A shared concern for their daughter. Eleven months late, but better than not knowing at all. An excited screech from the little girl reminded him that coming over here wasn't about bitterness and retribution. Or bonding with Emily. He was here to connect with Annie.

He made a noisy spectacle of opening the packaging of the doll to get her attention. She glanced over her shoulder and watched him with great interest. After several moments, she plopped on her bottom, then went on hands and knees into crawling mode. In nanoseconds, she'd made a beeline to him and fatherly pride at the little speeder filled him.

Cal glanced up at Em who smiled and nodded, indicating she understood and approved of his plan. It was a signal of cooperation and nice to know he had her support.

Annie crawled beside him and used the coffee table to stand up. She watched as he pulled the pink stuffed, terry-cloth-covered soft doll from the box and undid the excess of fasteners holding it in place on the cardboard.

"They don't make it easy, do they?" he grumbled.

"That's an understatement," Em agreed. She walked over and sat on the other side of the table, staying close by but in a neutral way.

Again Cal felt the cage of his resentment rattle and struggled to keep it from opening and slipping away. Where could he hide if it was gone? He finally freed the doll and set it on his knee where Annie could touch it. She rested a small hand on the sofa for balance and he realized that she was basically standing on her own.

"See that?" he asked Em.

"I know." She smiled tenderly. "But if she realizes it, she'll sit down. Physically she's capable of taking her first steps, but mentally not so much."

"She's ready to walk." Again fatherly pride in her accomplishment filled him even as he automatically screened her growth and development. "Right on schedule."

"Yup," she agreed. "Any day now I expect her to be walking. She's completely, blessedly normal."

"Normal's good." The downside of doing what he did was seeing the not normal stuff and again he felt the weight of responsibility to keep Annie's world perfectly ordinary.

She poked a tiny finger at the doll and started to babble, grunt and wiggle closer.

"I think she wants you to pick her up," Em said.

His gaze jumped to hers. "Really?"

"Yeah, she's a typical woman. Retail strategy works like a charm."

"Busted." He looked at his daughter. "Hey, Annie. What do you think about a vertical lift?"

He set the doll on the sofa beside him and put his hands around her middle, gently lifting her to his knee. When she instantly leaned forward but couldn't reach the toy, he handed it to her and she happily squeezed the pliable doll against her chest.

"And we have a successful mission," he said. "Contact without crying."

"Congratulations," Em said. "See, all it takes is time."

"That, and judicious use of a credit card."

"A stroke of genius."

And he rode the wave as far as it took him. For the next hour he opened the gifts he'd brought one by one and played with his little girl. She voluntarily crawled into his lap and handed him things, asking him to show her how they worked. He made her smile and laugh. It was a long time before she got grumpy and that behavior was accompanied by the rubbing of eyes, which meant she was tired.

"It's time for this little girl to go night night," Em said when Annie crawled into her arms and rested a head on her shoulder. "I'm going to change her and put her to bed."

She stood and stopped in the hallway before turning back. "You can come with us if you want."

He did and watched her competently and confidently diaper then rock Annie to sleep. Em put her on her back in the white crib with the pink princess sheets and blanket. After covering her to the waist, she turned on a night-light and led him back into the living room.

Cal didn't have the words to describe the excitement and exhilaration of holding his child and taking positive steps in gaining her trust. But trust didn't extend to he and Em.

"It's getting late, Cal." She opened the door. "Thanks for coming over."

"Thanks for letting me." He stopped in front of her, feeling the heat outside mix with the cool air within. When cold air mixed with hot, it created just the right conditions for a tornado.

This woman had a mouth made for kissing and he knew that from personal experience. He'd missed a lot about Emily after she walked away from their affair, and kissing was right at the top of that list. Apparently the adrenaline of euphoria was still pumping through him, which was the only explanation for what he did next.

Cal slid an arm around her waist and pulled her against him as he lowered his mouth to hers. The touch drained the tension he hadn't even realized was coiled inside him. He tasted surprise on her lips just before the surrender in a mix of tongue and teeth and teasing. Her breasts nestled against his chest, making him fervently wish they were skin to skin. His fingers found the hem of her shirt and he was just about to slide it up when she pressed her hands to his shoulders.

It was a signal, a negative one and not what his body was hoping for. In the combination of outside and inside light he could see that Em's pulse and heart rate were as elevated as his own and there was some satisfaction in that.

He stepped back and sucked air into his lungs before saying, "That was a combination thank-you and good-night."

"I knew that," she said, her voice husky and breathless at the same time.

"I'm going now."

"That would be best," she agreed.

"Thanks for letting me come over and not giving me a hard time for spoiling Annie."

"Good night, Cal."

After she shut the door, he realized the inherent problem with what just happened. She didn't believe his lame excuse for kissing her any more than he did.

Chapter Five

Emily had terminated her per diem status at the same hospital where Cal worked immediately after the disastrous conversation when she'd tried to tell him about her pregnancy. At the time she'd thought it the best thing, although she loved this hospital. Now that he knew about Annie, there was no reason to avoid him, and Em had activated her employment status at Mercy Medical Center.

Earlier that morning when she'd walked to the facility from the parking lot that overlooked Mercy Medical Center Parkway she realized how much she'd missed this place. The beautiful bell tower outside evoked spirituality and charm even before setting foot inside the building. In the lobby, a perfectly lighted painting of a single yellow rose and the inspirational words carved over graceful archways continued the theme of peace.

Within the walls of this hospital, the dedicated staff channeled the power of working together into healing the mind, body and spirit of the patients. Another thing she was beginning to realize was how much she'd missed Cal and seeing him at work. As a representative of social services, she was called in if there was a suspicion of child abuse, elder mistreatment or a financial need. She was on her way to the E.R. right now because Cal had asked for a social worker to see one of his patients.

Her mind should be on her work, but just the thought of Cal made her mouth tingle with memories of his kiss. A combination of good-night and thank-you, he'd said. It was less complicated to take him at his word, but their mouths had been way too familiar, way too eager, way too impatient for more, and the kiss had gone on far too long to believe the touch was that simple.

Her stomach knotted—a combination of nerves and anticipation. When the E.R.'s automatic doors whispered apart, she walked through them and saw him at the information desk, talking to the nurse manager. Rhonda angled her chin toward the entrance, and Cal glanced over his shoulder, before straightening to face her.

Emily stopped at the desk. "Hi, Rhonda. Cal."

The curvy, brown-eyed blonde nodded. "The name badge is a big clue that you're working."

"Yes. Social Services is understaffed because of vacations and called me in to help out."

"I see." Rhonda gave her a cool stare.

"Where's Annie?" Cal asked. "With Lucy? Or Patty?"

"Not exactly. They have work and school respectively. Annie's at Nooks and Nannies, a day-care center."

"So what happens to Oscar and Henry?"

"They're at the day-care center, too, while their moms are at work on-site. Ginger Davis, the president and director, runs a program on the UNLV campus that utilizes early childhood education students who get hours toward their certification to work in that field. She offers child care at a free or reduced rate for moms who qualify for assistance."

He didn't argue, but happy didn't come close to describing his expression. Glancing over his shoulder he said, "Weren't you on your way to lunch, Rhonda?"

"Was I?" she asked, looking from him to Em.

"You were, and I recommend sticking to that plan while things are quiet here. There's no one in the waiting room and you can't count on that to last very long." He nodded, a small movement that let her know he was okay. "The asthmatic is finally stabilized. I'm going to watch him a little longer to make sure he's okay before signing the discharge order."

"He doesn't need to be admitted?" she asked.

"Not this time. But he's had too many E.R. visits." He looked at Emily. "And that's what I need to talk to you about."

"Okay."

"I'll be back," Rhonda said, sliding off her chair.

Emily felt the wariness and missed the warm acquaintance she used to enjoy with Cal's right-hand gal. "Have a nice lunch, Rhonda."

Her only response was a quick wave before the woman rounded the corner to the cafeteria.

She looked up at Cal. Somehow the man managed to make the blue scrubs look less like pajamas and more like a sexy, heroic, knight-in-shining armor suit. But that would imply he was acting and the stethoscope he wore draped around his neck was a prop. Nothing could be further from the truth. He cared passionately about his small patients. And that was why he'd sent for her—not *her* specifically, but someone from Social Services.

"What can I do for you?" she asked.

His gaze darkened for a moment, like it had after their kiss. "It's the third time in ten days this kid's been in the E.R. for asthma. This time we just barely kept him from being admitted, and possibly put on a ventilator."

"How can I help?"

"The problem is that when he gets here the attack is so severe he needs immediate intervention because he hasn't used rescue meds. The family recently lost their medical insurance when Dad was laid off from his construction job."

Em remembered what he'd said about not wanting to see the same patients in the E.R. "What does the little guy need?"

"To learn how to manage the condition. The family has to understand that maintenance medications are necessary to stop an episode that could result in hospitalization, which is pretty traumatic, not to mention expensive. The ultimate goal is to minimize or prevent permanent lung damage."

She tapped her lip. "There's an asthma education program at the clinic where Henry and Oscar go. It's run by a pediatric pulmonologist. He does lung volume screenings as well as instruction for the parents or caregivers on how to deal with the illness so that the child can lead as normal a life as possible."

Cal nodded. "Who's the doc?"

"Nick Damien."

"I've worked with him. He's good." He thought for a moment. "Is there any cost?"

It was her job to know what programs and services were available in the community to meet the patient's needs when they left the hospital. Discharge planners were assigned to follow each admit to make sure care was given in a timely fashion to eliminate unnecessary cost. Because of Helping Hands and the girls she mentored, she had an even more personal knowledge of this particular program.

"The doc, and whatever staff he brings in, donate their

time and it's a free clinic. I'll check into it further and speak with the parents for you."

"Good."

"All right, then, I'll get right to it." She started to turn away and felt his hand on her arm.

"Wait, Em." He removed his fingers from her skin and curled them into his palm. "Since you're here, there's something else I'd like to run by you."

"Okay. Sure." She sounded like a nervous schoolgirl. Too eager. Too adoring. A puppy too anxious to please. It was that darn kiss. The good news was that she hadn't collapsed into bed with him, like the very first time he'd kissed her. The bad news? She had desperately *wanted* to collapse into bed with him.

He folded his arms over his chest and leaned against the high desk. "Look, I know you don't like the idea of moving into my house with Annie. But I've been thinking. What if I—"

"Don't even say it," she said, holding up a hand. "You can't live with us. How would that look? What kind of example would that set for the girls? It's out of the question."

"Okay." He blinked at her. "Actually I was going to ask how you'd feel about me throwing Annie a first birthday party. A family party. At my house." He watched her reaction for several moments before adding, "You shouldn't feel bad about thinking the worst of me."

"Why?"

He ran a finger down her hot cheek, just to show he didn't miss the embarrassment. "It will work in my favor."

"Oh?"

"When you feel guilty about going to the bad place, I'll probably get what I really wanted in the first place."

"You think so?"

"Before you say no, at least think about it."

He was probably right, because she had a lot to feel guilty

about and owed him. But letting down her guard wasn't easy. "This is all a big adjustment, considering that contrary to what you told me there really is a circumstance that would compel you to commit."

He blew out a breath and rested his hands on lean hips. "How much longer are you going to punish me for saying that?"

"Just stating the truth. We both made mistakes. But we have Annie to think about and I don't want to make any more where she's concerned. The thing is that I'd sort of figured to celebrate Annie's first birthday with the girls and their kids. Oscar and Henry aren't related by blood, but she's close to them."

"Lucy and Patty could come with the boys," he offered. "I'd also like to ask my folks. And my brother. I know it's probably not a good idea to overwhelm Annie with everyone at once, but since I've been making progress, I've been thinking that it's time she met her grandparents and the rest of her family."

Wouldn't *that* be fun? she thought. His E.R. manager already wanted to cut her heart out with a spoon and Em could only imagine how his parents felt. But Annie should know her whole family. "I really think that's—"

"Look, Em," he said, an irritated expression sliding into his eyes. "If you can keep finding speed bumps to the idea, I'm not opposed to playing the guilt card. I've missed out on a lot with Annie this first year of her life and so have my folks. They'd like to meet their granddaughter."

"Now who's going to the bad place? I was just going to say that it's a good idea. Annie deserves to meet everyone on your side of the family."

"Okay, then." He nodded as the tension seemed to drain out of him. "I'll get back to you with the details."

"Sounds good." Yeah, right. It wasn't easy to let him back in when she'd reconciled herself to the fact that he didn't want her or any responsibility that might come along with her. For Annie's sake she had to try. "Now I better go meet with your patient's family."

"Yeah." He started to lead the way to the trauma bay before turning back to her. "Do you have an appointment for your ultrasound yet?"

She nodded. "Right after Annie's birthday."

"That's two weeks. They can't get you in sooner?"

"The department is busy and I can't say I'm sorry to wait. Rebecca said two weeks won't impact the outcome, especially if it's benign as she suspects. If it's bad news, I don't want to know before Annie's big day. I'd rather be the queen of denial."

"All right," he said, uncertainty dark in his eyes.

He'd always wanted to fix things, and she recognized the impulse now in the look on his face. The expression was enough to send her to a place where Cal actually cared. Probably he did, but only because she was the mother of his child. Oh, how she wished it could be about her in a very personal way. But somehow she'd have to resolve that feeling and stop hoping for more than she had a right to expect from him.

Em turned left from Tropicana Avenue into Spanish Trail and stopped at the guard gate. After giving her name to the uniformed security guy, he checked his list and waved her through. She'd been feeling a huge, black dread about this day for the last two weeks, ever since she'd agreed to have Annie's first birthday party at Cal's place. On Sunday. With his family. What had she been thinking? It didn't matter what she'd thought. There had been no choice and here she was, on her way to family day.

There were a number of separate communities housed in this development—condominiums, all the way up to million-dollar houses. Cal had one of the latter and she knew it backed up to the golf course. Only the best for Mercy Medical's resident playboy.

After turning right, she navigated her way through the streets, remembering the route as if she'd visited only yesterday. The homes ranged from sprawling, stucco-covered ranch style to the lofty, two-story variety all fronted by sentinels of mature palm trees lining the streets. Her little compact, although in pristine condition and meticulously maintained, looked out of place when she passed driveways where Lexus, Mercedes and BMW vehicles lived. She'd been here many times, but had never before felt like the riffraff police would pull over and ask what she was doing there. It wasn't necessary to be a shrink to understand that this feeling was more about seeing Cal's family again.

He'd have told them the whole story. Em was the one who'd neglected to tell him about his daughter and expected they were less than pleased with how she'd handled the situation. Maybe it was the guilt police she should watch for in her rearview mirror.

She parked in front of his two-story, sprawling, white-stucco home with the red-tile roof. The expansive front yard was a combination of green grass and rocky desert landscaping, with a wooden bridge over a dry lake bed. It was perfect.

Em went to the rear passenger side of the car and gently unbuckled a dozing Annie from her car seat.

"Hey, big girl." Em smiled as her little one rubbed her eyes. "I'm glad you had a power nap. It's a big day for you. Not only are you a whole year old, you're going to meet your grandparents and your uncle Brad."

"Da?" Annie's big blue eyes opened wide.

"Yes. Daddy will be here. This is his house." The big, beautiful place where he wanted his daughter to live but

Mommy had put a big, fat no on the idea. "Mommy has good reasons. You might not understand when you see the impressive interior. But my reasons made perfect sense at the time. You have to trust Mommy."

"Da?" Annie pointed a pudgy finger at the house.

"Okay. We can do this."

Armed with a fully loaded diaper bag and her one-year-old daughter, Em marched up the driveway, past Cal's folks economical SUV and his brother's expensive, two-seater red Mercedes. Somehow she'd get through this, she thought, pulling on her emotional armor.

Beside the huge, double doors with oval etched-glass inserts was a button that she pushed to ring the bell. Annie leaned over to imitate the action, but Em held on tight, and then the door opened and Cal was there.

Annie blinked up at him and smiled. "Da?"

"Hey, sunshine." He held out his arms and the little girl eagerly went to him. He kissed her cheek as if he'd been doing it since the day she was born. "How's my girl?"

"Couldn't be better," Em answered for her.

He looked past her. "Where are Patty, Lucy and the boys?"

"They couldn't make it." Better to be vague than tell him what they really said. The invitation had pity written all over it and they'd feel uncomfortable. So Em was here without backup.

"Too bad. Maybe another time. The kids would enjoy the pool." He took the diaper bag, then backed up with Annie so she could come inside. "The folks are here."

"Yeah," she said, a knot in her stomach. "I noticed."

She followed him through the imposing, two-story-high entryway that divided the formal dining and living rooms. The family room and kitchen combination had been her favorite part of the house. It had been love at first sight, not unlike the way she'd once felt about Cal.

The remarkable amount of space didn't make the room any less inviting. A granite-covered island as big as a small country dominated the kitchen, which had a stainless-steel refrigerator, oven and dishwasher. Separating this from the family room was a bar with six stools. The walls were two-tone olive green with white chair rail dividing the light shade on top from the darker one on the bottom.

A big, overstuffed brown leather corner group filled one corner in front of a large-screen plasma TV. Neutral beige carpet flowed throughout the house making the already extraordinary floor plan seem even more spacious. The rectangular mahogany coffee table held a pile of presents in pink birthday paper.

Carol and Ken Westen were standing in front of the bar, with Brad beside them. Cal's brother was eighteen months younger and maybe an inch shorter, but still more than six feet tall with dark blond hair and blue eyes. Both of the Westen boys had gotten the cleft in their chins from Dad. Brad was just as good-looking as Cal, in an edgier, cockier way.

"Hello, Emily." Carol smiled, but it was tense around the edges. The boys had gotten their sandy blond hair from her, although mom's was lighter, thanks to regular coloring and highlights.

"Nice to see you again." Ken held out his hand, and she put hers into it. The man's hair was completely silver but only made him look more distinguished. He was probably in his late fifties but looked far younger and still handsome, a glimpse of how gracefully Cal would age. Probably his brother, too.

Brad cleared his throat. "Em," he said.

"Hi." She couldn't go wrong being succinct and polite.

She'd met Cal's family on numerous occasions. She knew how warm they could be and keenly felt the absence of it now.

"This is Annie," Cal said, grinning proudly.

"She's beautiful." Carol's blue eyes grew soft, tender and teary. "Cal says you named her after me and your mother."

Em nodded. "That's right. Ann Marie."

"Do you think she'll come to me?" Carol asked.

"She's a little shy at first," Cal said. "I had to bribe her. My daughter has a definite materialistic streak."

Em glanced around the room and its expensive furnishings. "And who do you think she gets it from?"

Brad laughed. "She's got you there, bro."

Carol held out her arms to her granddaughter and smiled warmly. "Hi, sweetheart. Will you let grandma hold you?" Annie went to her without hesitation and the older woman cuddled her close. "She's completely adorable."

Cal looked puzzled. "How come she didn't cry for you?"

"I think it's a guy thing," Em said. "She's a little standoffish with men."

"Way to go, Annie," Cal said. Uncle Brad and his father nodded approvingly.

"Do you think she'd like to go in the pool?" Carol asked.

"She loves her bath," Emily said, noticing for the first time that everyone was dressed for swimming, the older woman wearing a cover-up over her one-piece suit. "I brought her bathing suit and sunscreen and a hat."

Cal handed his mother the diaper bag. "Go for it, Mom."

"Is it all right with you, Emily?"

"Of course."

After getting Annie ready, Carol carried her outside followed by Cal and his brother. From where she stood, Em could see the crystal-clear pool, wrought-iron fence and the golf course with lake beyond. She followed more slowly to give them some space and took a padded chair in the shade of the patio cover complete with misters.

Ken offered her a cold drink, then sat beside her. "How've you been, Emily?"

"Fine. And you?"

"Good. Carol's been after me to slow down. She wants to do some traveling so I've added another doctor to my practice."

She knew his specialty was internal medicine. Both of his sons were doctors, but each had chosen different fields. "Do you have any trips planned?"

"We're taking a cruise to Alaska. Always said we wanted to go where it was cold when Vegas was hotter than the face of the sun."

Em wouldn't have thought it possible, but she laughed. "When are you going?"

"In September. We're flying to Juneau, catching the boat for a repositioning cruise that goes to San Diego and winds up in L.A."

He was watching his wife bounce the laughing baby in the pool while Cal and Brad stood by like vigilant guardians. Em had to admit that Annie's father was really something. Tall, tan, fit and fine. His broad shoulders tapered to a trim waist and flat belly. The dusting of hair on his chest brought back memories of twisted sheets and tantalizing touches. Her heart skipped once, then speeded up and suddenly *she* was hotter than the face of the sun.

She swallowed and pushed the image from her mind. Focus, she told herself. "The trip sounds wonderful."

"Not as wonderful as finding out we have a grandchild."

She glanced at him and didn't see hostility. "Yes, sir, about that. If you'll let me explain—"

"Cal told us."

"Everything?"

"He said you raised the subject of children and he cut you off with a speech about going it alone."

"That's the truth, Mr. Westen."

"You sound surprised."

"I guess I am. I wouldn't blame Cal if he embellished and painted me in a bad light."

"Cal's a stickler for the truth, even if he doesn't get the sympathy vote on this one. And you used to call me Ken," he reminded her.

"That was before I didn't tell your son he was a father. But," she added, "I had my reasons." She glanced at him. "In my past, there are some things I—I'd rather not talk about."

"I understand." He nodded. "And you'll understand that Cal has a past, too."

Em held the soda can tightly in her hands and felt the aluminum give way. "Doesn't everyone?"

"Some more than others." He met her gaze. "Did he tell you about his marriage?"

Cal married? Mercy Medical's playboy had once taken the plunge? He'd only told her he wasn't married and she'd assumed that meant he'd *never* tied the knot. "No. He never mentioned it."

Ken took a sip of his soda. "That doesn't surprise me."

"Why?"

"Since he's no longer married, you can assume it didn't go well," he said wryly.

"What happened?" She wanted to ask what the woman had done to him that made him avoid commitment like radioactive fallout. It would explain a lot about why he'd shut her down tight as a high-rise during a bomb threat.

"The fact that he didn't say anything to you would imply that it's still too painful for him to talk about." Ken met her gaze. "I've probably said too much already. It's Cal's story to tell. Or not."

She nodded even though curiosity was clawing through her.

She looked at Cal, taking Annie from his mom and lifting her high to make her giggle, then lowering her slowly into the water where she splashed happily. Clearly when he'd said nothing could compel him to commit, he hadn't meant a child.

"I should have told him anyway," she said softly. "I—I didn't mean to hurt him. Or you. And Mrs. Westen."

"We were surprised. And hurt that we missed her beginning." Ken looked over and his expression was filled with gentle censure. "But for Annie's sake we all need to put that behind us and move forward."

"Can you?" she asked.

"Time will tell."

"Fair enough."

And she sincerely meant that.

Em had expected animosity and accusation but Cal's family was trying. And she could tell by the way they looked at Annie that it was love at first sight with the little girl. Cal's little girl. The child of their child.

A peace swept over her for the first time since she'd found the lump. If anything happened to her she knew Annie would be loved and cared for. No matter what happened, her little girl would have the family that Emily had only ever been able to dream about.

Among other dreams. One of which was kissing Cal again even though it was a red-flag warning of fire danger. Telling him the truth had eliminated her worry about Annie's future. Unfortunately it was replaced by concern about her own and how in the world she would handle him being in her life again.

Chapter Six

The day after his daughter's first birthday party, Cal sat across from his two medical practice partners—Mitch Tenney and Jake Andrews. Once a month they got together for a status meeting and normally he looked forward to it. Not today. The problem was, his mind was working less on the professional and more on the personal.

After Em had left his house with Annie, he and his dad had a long talk. Ken had told him he needed to put the past away for good and concentrate on his daughter. Forgive and forget.

"Not happening," Cal mumbled.

"Are you paying attention?" Mitch Tenney demanded.

Cal sat up straighter. "Yes."

"You're lying," his partner accused, dark blue eyes intense. But that wasn't cause for alarm. Mitch was always intense so it was situation normal. "Otherwise you'd be on board with holding up your end of responsibility in this practice when Mercy Medical Center opens the third hospital campus next year."

"What are you talking about?" Cal asked.

He looked across the mahogany table at Jake Andrews, his other friend and the man responsible for pulling he and Mitch into this trauma group. The three of them were more than partners. They'd met when Cal and Mitch began their residency in trauma intervention at the county hospital in Las Vegas. Jake had been finishing up his surgical residency at the facility and they all clicked.

Jake came up with the idea of pooling their talents for the practice and their business association began. Cal and Mitch contracted their services to Mercy Medical Center to staff the E.R. and Jake was called in when surgical intervention was necessary to save a life.

Mitch pointed to the typed agendas on the table. "Pay attention. We have things to discuss."

"Yes, Mother," Cal said, saluting sharply.

Not so long ago Mitch Tenney had been a bullet point on the monthly agenda, in hot water for his no-holds-barred, straight-forward, take-no-prisoners style of practicing medicine. He said what he thought and let the chips fall where they may. Arnold Ryan, Mercy Medical's hospital administrator, had made a lot of noise about not renewing their contract. The situation had since been resolved with conflict-resolution counseling.

"Stand down, guys," Jake said, gray eyes serious.

They called him Dr. GQ, and not just because of his beach-resort tan and tautly toned abs. You could fry an egg on the sidewalk outside, but Jake Andrews didn't know the meaning of casual. He wore a crisp white dress shirt, an expensive red silk tie and black slacks that could be Armani. Every dark brown hair was in place thanks to haircuts in the four-hundred-dollars-a-pop range.

"We've got business to discuss," he added. "And the next order of business is recruiting for the practice. With the new Mercy Medical campus opening, we need to find a couple of quality docs or kiss a personal life goodbye."

Cal's personal life wasn't in the best shape anyway and a kiss goodbye could be a good thing. Then again, time with Annie was a priority now. "The county hospital where we trained is a good place to start looking."

Jake nodded. "I agree. So who's going to take the lead on that?"

"I thought you were." Mitch pulled his pager out of his blue scrubs shirt pocket and checked the display, then replaced it. "After all, you showed impeccable judgment with Cal and I."

"And it's a good thing humility wasn't the decisive factor." Jake tapped his Mont Blanc pen on the legal pad in front of him. "Maybe one of you could step up and take point on personnel? Mitch? You're not on probation anymore."

"Oh, for Pete's sake. Am I ever going to live that down?"

"No," his two friends said together. Jake added, "It's carved in stone on our agenda."

"Look," Mitch said, resting his forearms on the table. "That particular problem is old news. I'm making nice with everyone at the hospital from staff to the administrator."

"It helps," Cal pointed out, "when the administrator in question is your father-in-law."

Mitch grinned the grin that made women far and wide regret that he was off the dating market. "He isn't such a bad guy."

"Since when?" Jake wanted to know.

"Since he's going to be a grandfather any day now. Sam put him on notice. If he wants a relationship with his daughter and grandchild, he has to be on his best behavior."

"So you're hiding behind a woman's skirts?" Cal clarified.

"As long as my wife is wearing it, you bet I am," Mitch

declared. "I'm going on record here—impending grandfa-
therhood has mellowed Arnold Ryan."

Samantha Ryan Tenney had been Mitch's conflict-resolution counselor and during those first few weeks they did
more than discuss his attitude. The two had only been
married a couple of months, but were expecting their baby
any day now.

"How is Sam?" Cal asked.

"She's retaining enough water in her ankles to float the
largest aircraft carrier in the Pacific fleet," he answered. "Her
words, not mine."

"Wow." Cal stared in amazement. "She's really good at her
job, isn't she? There's no other explanation for this diplomatic
streak you've got going."

"Bite me," Mitch said grinning. "Seriously, she's healthy
and Rebecca—"

"Rebecca Hamilton? The ob-gyn?" Cal wanted to know.

"Yeah. She says the baby is fine and will come in his own
good time."

"It's a boy?" Jake asked.

"Of course."

Cal looked at him. "Do you know for sure?"

"Sam wants to be surprised. But I know," he said.

"Because?" Cal pushed.

"I want a boy."

"What's wrong with a girl?" Cal demanded.

"Absolutely nothing. But Sam knows that my preference
is a boy first."

"And when you say jump, Sam asks how high?" Jake
wanted to know.

"Hardly." Mitch laughed ruefully. "But we've talked about
a boy first who can look after a little sister."

Interesting, Cal thought. "You want more kids?"

"We have to get through this one," Mitch said, intensity sneaking back into his eyes.

"You're a nervous father-to-be," Jake commented, sounding surprised.

"What's there to be nervous about? I'm a doctor and childbirth is the most natural thing in the world." Mitch checked his pager again. "Hell, yes, I'm nervous. I've never done this before—expecting a baby, I mean. I've delivered them. I treat patients who come into the emergency room and I'm pretty darn good at that. But the situation is different when you're emotionally invested. Training, intelligence and common sense go right out the window when someone you love is involved."

Cal knew exactly what he meant. His medical specialty was pediatric emergency intervention, but when it came to Annie, training didn't take away the tightness in his chest. He wondered how he would have felt if he'd known Emily was pregnant with Annie. He'd have been there when his child was born. That much he knew. But Em had cheated him out of the chance to be excited ahead of time and he never had the opportunity to hand out cigars along with the news of his firstborn. The option of whether or not to find out if she was a boy or a girl had been stolen along with the experience of being surprised. Would he have been nervous? He'd never know.

"So," Jake said to their partner, "you're going to be a father soon. I guess you'll be a little too busy to take on the project of adding docs to the practice." He looked at Cal. "That leaves you."

Cal nodded. "I'll help out with that. But—"

"What?" Jake asked, eyes narrowing.

"You're the heart and soul of this medical practice," Cal said. "I'm a little surprised that you're delegating."

"Funny you should say that. I'll be campaigning for the position of Trauma Medical Director at the new Mercy Medical campus." Jake put the pricey pen down and looked at them, waiting for a reaction.

Cal grinned at him. "You're the best trauma surgeon in the valley. The medical board would be crazy not to appoint you."

"I'm not the only candidate. There's some talented competition," Jake said.

"You'll get it," Mitch predicted. "And when you do this group's standing in the medical community will do some serious kick-ass upward mobility."

"Not bad for a boy from the wrong side of the tracks."

Jake's softly spoken comment probably wasn't meant to be heard, and both Mitch and Cal didn't question him. None of them talked much about what happened before they met. There was something about life-and-death trauma that made you live in the now.

"So," Jake said, "you'll both help with recruiting as much as possible?" When they agreed to that, he looked down at the notes in front of him. "Then I guess that about covers this meeting. Is there any other business?"

"Yeah."

Cal looked at his friends. He hadn't planned to talk about what was going on with him, but he had a child to think about and that would impact his available time for the "as much as possible" part of recruiting for the practice. His partners had a right to know. "I need to tell you why I'm reluctant to commit a lot of time for vetting new doctors."

"You mean other than cutting into your time with the ladies?" Mitch said.

"One lady in particular," Cal clarified.

"One? You're abandoning the 'axis of attraction'?" Jake asked, referring to their nickname at Mercy Medical Center. At least it had been.

"Technically, Mitch already deserted the bachelor ranks,"

Cal reminded him. "And the female I'm talking about isn't a lady yet. She's my daughter and just turned one."

It wasn't often his partners were rendered speechless, but they were now.

Jake tugged on his ear. "I'm sorry. It sounded like you just said you have a one-year-old."

"I do. Her name is Annie."

"Does she have a mother?" Mitch asked.

"Emily Summers."

The two of them speechless twice in less than a minute must be some kind of a world record.

"I always liked Emily," Jake finally said.

"Me, too." Mitch looked at his pager, then slid it back into his pocket. "And when things didn't work out with the two of you, I wondered what you did to scare her off."

"What makes you think it was me?" Cal demanded.

"Because you're you. And Em is one of the good ones." Jake leaned back in his chair. "Now that the two of you are together and you're off the market, I'm the lone holdout. Single and—"

"Sassy," Cal said sarcastically. "But here's the thing—Em and I aren't together. She came to me a couple weeks ago and told me that she had my baby." Her medical reasons for doing it were private and not something he would share without her permission. "I'm waiting for DNA confirmation, but the resemblance to my side of the family is pretty convincing evidence."

"I repeat that Em is one of the good guys," Jake said. "And the fact that you're thinking in terms of personal time management means that if not off the market, you're at least embracing the spirit of it—being a father, I mean."

"Congratulations," Mitch said. "I can't believe you beat me to it."

And Cal couldn't believe his friends hadn't exhibited

manly outrage on his behalf. He'd been lied to, but they seemed genuinely pleased that Em was back in his life. He was struggling with that himself because of some rogue gene that made him want her so badly, in spite of everything she'd done.

What to do with an ailing, aging parent was a social service that fell into Em's sphere of expertise. She left the E.R. where she'd met with the patient and family, giving them information on skilled nursing and hospice facilities, as well as facts about finances and programs available to offset some of the cost.

It seemed like the eighty-eight-year-old's son and his wife were more at peace than when Em had first entered the room and they hadn't any idea where to turn for help. Knowledge was power and she knew from firsthand experience that having no power over a situation could be a black pit of despair.

Walking down a long, tiled corridor away from the E.R. toward the elevator, she heard footsteps behind her.

Then a man's questioning voice. "Emily?"

She slowed her step and turned, recognizing the doctor instantly. That's when she braced herself. "Jake. Hi."

He stopped in front of her. "It's been a while."

"Yeah." Had he stopped her to tell her off? Cal's partners were protective of each other. Did Jake know she'd kept the information about Cal's child from him? His expression gave no clue to his state of mind.

Jake Andrews had Hollywood looks and could play a doctor on TV if he wasn't the real thing in real life. He was tall, dark and handsome with eyes that were both serious and mysterious. Most physicians dressed casually when making rounds at the hospital, but not Jake. He was wearing a dark charcoal suit, gray shirt that matched his eyes and a black and silver silk tie. Em had always wondered what his story was. He was too nice, too good-looking, too perfect. And too alone.

She knew something about isolating oneself to keep secrets. The same instincts that made her a good social worker told her that Dr. Incredible was hiding something.

"How long have you been back to work at Mercy Medical Center?" he asked.

"Just a couple weeks." Since not having to avoid Cal any longer.

"Cal, Mitch and I were just talking about you."

"Oh?"

She shouldn't mind what Cal's friends thought, but that didn't stop her. During the time they'd been together, she'd spent a lot of time with Mitch Tenney and Jake Andrews, long enough to like and respect the two dedicated docs. Long enough to talk herself into believing that a man who hung out with the good guys could be one himself. One who could care about her. Learning she'd been wrong had been a bitter pill to swallow.

Jake slid his hands into his slacks' pockets. "I hear congratulations are in order for you and Cal. So... Belated congrats on your daughter."

"Thank you." Defensive words marched through her mind, but she managed not to let any of them out. "Annie is a blessing and a joy."

"One you didn't see fit to share with her father. Until now." Disapproval hardened his jaw and mouth. "What the hell were you thinking, Em? That's something a guy needs to know."

"I understand that. Now." She drew in a shuddering breath. "But when I tried to tell him I was pregnant, everything he said convinced me that he didn't want kids. The words stuck in my throat."

"How come now?"

Obviously Cal hadn't told his partners about her health concerns. It was her information to share and she did. "I have a lump in my breast. Something like that makes you realize stuff happens and if I wasn't around, Annie would be alone."

"I see." He was quiet for several moments, processing her words, deciding what to say. "Have you had it checked out?"

She nodded. "I'm scheduled for an ultrasound this Friday."

"Good."

"Look, Jake, I know now that it was a bad idea to keep Annie from Cal. I have my reasons, but that doesn't justify not telling him he was going to be a father. All I can do is my best to right the wrong."

"Okay."

"It's hard not to judge, I know." She shook her head. "But put yourself in my shoes."

One corner of his mouth quirked up. "Anatomically speaking, I can never walk in your shoes."

"Right. Let me elaborate. I was drowning in hormones, morning sickness lasted twenty-four hours a day, all of which made me an emotional wreck." She sighed. "Anyway, I handled it badly and Cal is resentful. Great with his daughter, but not so much with me. Although I can't really blame him."

"Look, Em—" Jake touched a hand to his impeccably knotted tie. "I'll deny saying this if anyone asks, but Cal isn't as tough as he pretends."

"What do you mean?"

"I can't give you specifics partly because he's my friend. Mostly because I don't know any."

She folded her arms over her chest as she looked up at him. "He's your friend and you have no details?"

"I'm a guy." He shrugged. "We don't talk about everything or pry into each other's lives. I just know that he was going through a rough time when I first met him."

"What kind of a rough time?"

"Like I said, I have no details and wouldn't give them up if I did. But when he started his residency at the county hospital, his wife was brought into the E.R.—"

"Wife?" she interrupted. What his dad said had been the first she'd heard about Cal's previous marriage. Since then curiosity about it had been her new best friend.

"Look, all I know is that he had personal problems before the divorce. So don't be too hard on him."

"Maybe you should do the same and not be too hard on me?" she asked. "For the record I want to be a guy and not talk about stuff."

He grinned. "Fair enough. It's really good to have you back, Em."

"Thanks. I've missed Mercy Medical Center."

"The feeling is mutual." For the first time, warmth crept into his eyes. "And you're a mom."

"Yeah. Can you believe it?"

"Absolutely. What's hard to wrap my head around is Cal Westen being a dad."

Tenderness welled up inside her. "He's so wonderful with Annie. She was standoffish at first, but persistence is his middle name."

"I've noticed that about him."

"He bought out the toy store and that got his daughter's attention in a big way."

Jake laughed. "I bet it did."

"He was very up front about spoiling her rotten in his campaign to win her affections."

"Good for him." He glanced at the TAG Heuer watch on his wrist and frowned. "I have to get going. A meeting—"

"Sorry. I didn't mean to talk your ear off."

"I'm glad I ran into you and cleared the air. There are two

sides to every story." He took a step forward and gave her a hug. "I'll look forward to seeing you—"

"Seeing her when?"

Em disengaged from Jake and turned toward the familiar deep voice. "Cal, I was—"

"Saying hi to my partner," he said.

Em wasn't sure why the hostility in his tone should make her feel guilty, but it did and the explanation came pouring out. "I was in the E.R. talking to some clients and ran into Jake on the way back to my office."

"Really?" Cal crossed his arms over his chest, and the sleeves of his scrubs pulled tight around the muscles in his upper arms.

The attitude and posture made her heart sing, which was crazy. But true.

"Yeah," Jake said. "Em was just telling me about your daughter."

"Was she?" He glanced down at her.

"And I was telling Jake what a terrific father you are," she said.

"I see." The tone said he didn't see at all.

Jake frowned. "Someone's having a bad day. People aren't playing nice?"

"Maybe too nice," Cal muttered, glaring at his friend.

"If you'd gone into surgery instead of the medical end, the people you interact with would be anesthetized," Jake pointed out.

"So you've mentioned more than once."

"My advice is an attitude adjustment," Jake said, grinning at his friend. Apparently he was accustomed to Cal's rotten moods. "Call me if surgery is required, but right now I'm late for a meeting with the hospital board. Bye, Em."

"Good to see you, Jake." She watched him walk down the hallway and turn right at the next corridor. Then she looked up at Cal and tried to think of something innocuous to say. "Annie had a good time at your house on Sunday."

"I'm glad." He ran his fingers through his hair, then met her gaze. "My folks are pretty happy about being grandparents."

"They're really great with her." Which must be where their son acquired the skill. "She really likes the toy tea cart they gave her."

"Oh?"

Em smiled up at him. "She loves pushing the thing around. It helps with her balance and walking. Just a little girly girl."

He hadn't smiled once since seeing her with Jake and in fact frowned harder. "Where is Annie, by the way?"

"Nooks and Nannies, the day-care center."

"What do you know about that place?"

"I already told you." She stared at him, wondering what set of circumstances had inoculated him against trusting.

"Are there security cameras on premises?"

She blinked at him. "What? For a hidden-camera investigation? Breaking news on Channel three?"

"Better safe than sorry."

"As a matter of fact, better than a camera, I have Lucy and Patty. I already told you they work there in exchange for child care while they're in classes."

"Busy girls."

"Busy *moms,*" she said pointedly. "For your information, I found the place through my friend Sophia Green who also works there. We've been through this already. I thought you were convinced that I'd never put Annie anywhere that I wasn't absolutely certain is a safe environment."

She didn't know whether to strangle him for being unreasonable, or kiss him for caring so much about his child.

The angry expression on his face didn't budge. "Did Jake ask you out?"

"What?"

"When I walked up I heard him say that he was looking forward to seeing you. Did he ask you out?"

"You're jealous?"

"Of course not," he said, just a little too forcefully. "But I know him. So many women, so little time."

He *was* jealous, Em realized, understanding why her heart had started to sing. But what did it mean? Surely jealousy was a good thing given that she couldn't seem to get him out of her mind.

But this wasn't the time or place.

"Look, Cal, I have to go. I have an appointment."

"The same one Jake has?" he asked.

She shook her head. "Mine is personal. I'll tell you about it later."

He had that stubborn look. "Em—"

She held up a hand to stop the questions. "Are you coming by to see Annie after work?"

"Yes."

"I'll tell you about it then."

She turned away before he could interrogate her further and found that distance didn't snuff out the sparklers going off inside her.

She'd struggled not to let hope in. She'd fretted about setting herself up for a fall. But herself had seen the evidence that Cal was jealous and no warning in the world could douse the radiance shining inside her.

Chapter Seven

Cal couldn't believe his partner had hit on Emily. What was up with that? One minute he was moaning about the axis of attraction falling apart, the next he was flexing those axis muscles in the hospital hallway. Every time he got a mental picture of her in Jake's arms, he wanted to deck Dr. GQ.

He pulled "the princess" to a stop in front of the empty field across from Em's apartment. He said when he got off work he'd see her later. Not her. Annie. And here he was to see his daughter. The only other car parked there was an old SUV that he knew belonged to Patty's boyfriend. Jake Andrews's expensive Lexus sedan was nowhere in sight.

Not that Cal was checking up. Em had a right to see whoever she wanted. But damn it to hell, he hated that the thought of her with another man tied him in knots.

He walked across the street and knocked on the door instead of ringing the bell in case Annie was asleep. Funny how such a little person could make so big a change in his life. Make him feel responsible and not care that he did. Make him feel protective—about his daughter's mother, too. But he preferred to believe his over-the-top reaction about Em dating had more to do with another guy being around his little girl. Part of him actually believed that. The other part recognized the lie because he'd never been able to get Em out of his system.

The door opened and there she was, wearing white shorts that made her shapely, tanned legs look amazing. Her hot pink cropped top revealed a line of skin that winked in and out when she moved. Pulling his self-control into place with an effort, he forced his gaze away from her tempting bare skin and up to her eyes.

"Hi." His voice sounded as rusty as an ancient garden gate and he hoped she didn't notice.

She lifted a hand, then put a finger to her lips for quiet. "Annie just fell asleep," she whispered, an erotic sound to his pent-up sexual frustration.

The pitch shouldn't have been seductive, but it made his hands tingle and the blood roared in his ears. Fortunately it wasn't a sound that would wake his daughter. "Is she okay?"

"Yeah. A day at day care always wears her out."

"I'm sorry I missed seeing her." In part because now there was no reason to stay. No cover story for hanging out with Em. And every cell in his body was begging him to hang out with her because he was aching to get her naked. "I'll just go—"

"Wait— There's something I need to talk to you about. It's serious and I'm glad she's asleep so we won't be interrupted."

"Okay." He swallowed hard as he walked in and she shut the door behind him. "What's up?"

"I wanted to tell you not to be jealous of Jake."

"I'm not jealous," he lied. And her words didn't begin to unknot the knot in his gut. "But okay."

"He's just a friend," she explained.

Not the time for him to mention Jake saying he'd always liked her. "Got it."

"Even if he was interested in me, which he's not, I could never think of him as anything but a friend."

"Good to know. And the thought never crossed my mind."

"I know that's a lie. Mostly because of your question about whether or not he'd asked me out. I'd never cause a problem between you and Jake. Just wanted you to know that there's absolutely no reason for you to be jealous of him."

"Okay, then." This conversation wasn't helping his frame of mind. "If there's nothing else, I'll just hit the road—" He cocked his thumb in the general direction of the front door behind him.

"Actually, that isn't all I wanted to say." She looked up at him and ran her tongue over her full, plump lips.

Cal held in a groan. Just barely. But there wasn't a guy on the planet who wouldn't be turned on. That was the sexiest damn thing he'd ever seen.

"What else is on your mind?" he managed to ask.

"About my appointment today?"

She'd told him about that, and he'd accused her of meeting Jake. He'd made an ass of himself earlier and she was going to make him regret it. "What about it?"

"I went to see an attorney."

That's not what he'd expected her to say. "Why? Is there a problem?"

"No. I just wanted you to know that I'm taking legal steps to ensure that you're recognized as her father and guardian. When the DNA test is back, we'll make sure he has the results."

"It's not necessary. No one has any doubt anymore that she's mine."

"I know. But I want to be certain that there are no loopholes. I want every *I* dotted and every *T* crossed." She twisted her fingers together. "He's going to handle the paperwork necessary to put your name on her birth certificate. We'll have to go to court and appear before a judge to finalize our joint custody of Annie."

"I can't believe you did that."

"It's true." She lifted one slender shoulder in a shrug. "I misjudged you. It doesn't matter that I was scared and seriously hormonal. No excuses. I'm just trying to make it right. For our daughter."

Cal had been wondering how to bring up the legalities of all this with her and was surprised, in a good way, that she'd acted without pressure from him. And so quickly. He was really happy.

For a couple of seconds, he grinned like a fool, then put his arms around her, lifted and swung her around. "That's pretty awesome," he said.

They laughed together and the thought crossed his mind that he might have reacted like this at the news that she was having his baby. But probably not. A woman had once told him that and it was a lie.

But wanting Em wasn't.

With her arms around his neck and her curves pressed against him, he couldn't deny that she felt good and right, like she belonged there. And always had. He'd missed her and having her back in his arms made him realize just how much.

He slowed the circling and stopped, staring into her dark eyes. Their mouths were too close and hers looked soft and sexy with her full lips slightly parted, as if she were waiting for him to taste her. The small, firm breasts that he'd loved loving a lifetime ago were burning into his chest. His breathing grew labored, but not from turning with the weight of her in his arms. The weight of her was a turn on, plain and simple.

He swallowed, the ache for her growing into a black hole inside him. A ripple of need fueled by electricity shocked him and he felt a shudder go through her, too, a shivery current that bounced back and forth between them.

And just like that the lonely months of being without her disappeared and it was like second nature to touch his lips to hers. Warm didn't begin to describe the sensation. Hot. It was hot and wet and… Wow. Then he heard her moan, a sound of pure pleasure that crushed out rational thought and he knew the waiting was done.

He couldn't fight the want and need any longer knowing she wanted and needed him, too.

He let her slide down his front until her feet touched the floor, then turned and pressed her against the wall, holding her there with his lower body as she arched her hips into his. He threaded his fingers in her hair as he kissed her over and over, chest pounding, her breathy moans pumping through him.

She smelled so good and felt like heaven. She was so soft, so curvy and so much woman that any idea of *not* touching her bare skin went straight out the window. He settled his hands on the line of skin that had tormented him since the second she'd opened the door. The feel of her flesh was like a shot of adrenaline straight to his heart.

He slid his hands up higher until he found her breasts in his palms and was pathetically grateful that she wasn't wearing a bra. He brushed his thumbs over her nipples and felt them pebble and grow hard. The sensation drove him crazy and all he could think about was being inside her.

After unfastening her shorts, he pushed them down and over her hips until they dropped to the floor. She reached out and unbuckled the belt on his jeans, then fumbled with the button and zipper before he pushed them down. He managed to yank out his wallet and snag the condom he always kept there, then roll it on. The next thing he knew, her legs were locked around his hips and he was buried inside her.

With his arms around her, he protected her back from the hard wall as he thrust into her over and over. Her breath came in gasps as she met each push until her body stilled and she clung to him while a series of shudders gripped her. With one final thrust, he joined her in release and groaned out his satisfaction.

For several moments they just held on to each other, struggling to get their breath. Finally he lifted his head and she let her legs slide down.

He stared at her. "I didn't come over here for that, but I'd be lying if I said I was sorry."

"I know." She dragged in air. "I'm not quite sure what to say."

"Then let's not—" He wasn't sure what they shouldn't do, but she nodded agreement. "I'll just go and—"

A cry from down the hall interrupted him and he felt Em's relaxed muscles go tight as she straightened.

"Annie—" She looked up at him. "Sometimes when she goes to sleep this early, it's just a nap and she's not in for the night."

"There's nothing wrong?" There were so many things wrong right now that he'd lost count, but he meant with his daughter.

Em shook her head. "I don't think so, but I'll go check on her."

She scrambled into her panties and shorts and straightened her top. Hot pink. That was prophetic. Hot didn't begin to describe what he'd felt. Being with Em just now ranked as the best sex of his life, which should make him more relaxed than he'd ever been. Not so much. Instead of taking the edge off, he was even more keyed up. He had more questions than answers. Including why even reminding himself about the woman who'd lied to him in his past hadn't stopped him from making love with the woman who'd lied in his present.

* * *

Em sat in the glider chair in Annie's bedroom, giving the baby a bottle while Cal sat on the ottoman in front of them and watched. Twenty minutes ago she'd lost control and made love with him. That was *intimacy.* But now—father, mother, baby—the three of them together, that was intimate in a solid, normal, *family* way.

This was a moment she'd never expected to have, especially because she'd thought he would disappear after getting what he wanted. But maybe he wanted more than that. A jealous man wasn't indifferent and it was possible that he could want both her and his daughter.

"So you're still bringing Annie over to my house for a swim on Saturday?"

Em nodded. "She loved the water so much on her birthday."

"Good. I'll look forward to it."

"Me, too."

She looked down and noticed their little water baby had stopped sucking on her bottle and milk dribbled down the side of her mouth. Taking the soft burp diaper she kept handy, Em wiped the moisture away. She started to set the bottle on the dresser beside her but Cal held out his hand.

"Thanks," she whispered, and kept gliding back and forth.

"Are you going to put her in the crib?"

"In a few minutes. If I don't wait until she's sound asleep, she'll be wide awake. And after a power nap, it could be a long time before she settles down again."

He shook his head. "It's amazing."

"What?"

"Everything." His big body made the ottoman look really small, and uncomfortable. He rested his elbows on his wide-spread knees and held the bottle in his hands.

She smiled and knew there was a trace of tenderness in it. "Define everything."

"Annie's world. All you know about her. Likes and dislikes. How to handle every situation. Her personality. The fact that she might not go right back to sleep if the stars and planets aren't perfectly aligned."

"That's just the tiniest bit dramatic."

"But you know what I mean."

She did. He'd missed out on that part of the parental learning curve. Guilt shot through her even though she'd promised herself to let it go. "Actually I pay attention because I'm selfish and lazy."

He looked surprised. "You might want to explain that."

"My job is easier if she's happy. I remember what she likes and doesn't like so that she eats and sleeps and is healthy."

"Ah. So it has nothing to do with loving her a lot."

"Of course not," she teased back. "And that's a big fat lie. I love her more than I can even put into words. How can you not love your own baby?"

"Yeah." He reached out and ran a finger over Annie's chubby arm. "What happened when she was born?"

"I went into labor. Twelve hours, by the way. It was uncomfortable, then I pushed and she came out." She shrugged.

"Smart aleck." He gave her a wry look. "I meant was anyone with you?"

How diplomatic. What he wanted to know was whether or not she was alone. "Sophia."

"Who's she?"

"Sophia Green, a social worker friend of mine. She manages the Nanny Network child-care center. She drove me to the hospital when my water broke and stuck around through labor and delivery. She was my Lamaze coach and continues to be my friend."

She thought it best not to mention just now that Sophia had convinced her to tell Cal about Annie after finding the breast lump.

"What about your mother?"

Emily had told him she and her mother weren't close but no details. "Mom passed away before Annie was born. It wasn't unexpected."

"Was she ill?"

"Yes. Cancer. And it didn't help that alcohol was her main source of nutrition for as long as I can remember."

"I'm sorry."

"Don't be. She doesn't deserve it."

Again he looked surprised. "Do you want to talk about it?"

"What?"

"Why you're so angry with her," he said.

"She's gone. There's nothing to say."

He looked surprised. "I've never known you to be anything but caring and concerned. This is different. I'm a good listener."

"Right. Wonder Doc, the golden boy of Mercy Medical Center gets in touch with his feminine side."

"Joke if you want. It's a defense mechanism." He set the baby bottle on the rug beside him, then linked his fingers together. "And for the record, a good doctor listens first before doing anything. Otherwise there's no way to figure out what's wrong."

Just when she was starting to feel good about him, her, Annie and the future, he had to bring up the past she was desperately trying to forget. "You don't really want to hear this."

He studied her. "I think you don't really want to tell it."

"Wonder Doc strikes again," she said. He *was* good.

"So tell me what happened. You'll feel better."

"How about if I take two aspirin and call you in the morning?"

He smiled. "You're stalling."

"Right again." She shifted Annie more comfortably in her arms. "You're not going to drop this, are you?"

"If you insist. But they say confession is good for the soul."

She softly kissed her daughter's forehead before looking

at Cal. Maybe he was right. More important, he *was* a doctor. He cared deeply about kids and wanted a good outcome for his patients. And now he had his own child. Clearly he had Annie's best interests at heart. Surely he would understand that all those years ago the welfare of her baby was why she'd made the most difficult, painful decision of her life? It finally felt safe to tell someone about what she'd gone through.

After taking a deep breath, she said, "I got pregnant when I was fifteen years old."

Em had never quite understood the meaning of pregnant pause until now. Clearly that declaration had stunned him into speechlessness and she didn't plan to fill the void with words.

"What happened?" he finally asked.

"My mother told me that she couldn't even afford to take care of me. No way could I bring a baby into the house for her to support. She gave me an ultimatum to give the baby up for adoption or find another place to live."

"So you gave your child away?"

She winced at the censure in his voice. "I ran away."

"To a friend's house? What about the baby's father?"

"After I told him I was pregnant, I never saw him again." She shook her head. "My own father was never in the picture. At that time being raised by a single mother who disappeared from reality into a cheap bottle of wine didn't help you fit in. Friends are hard to come by when you're different from everyone else."

"Where did you go?"

A chill went down her spine and she shivered. To this day she embraced the desert's summer heat and loathed the weeks of bitter cold that the chamber of commerce didn't advertise. "I had nowhere to go. I lived on the street."

"I don't understand—"

"Then let me spell it out. I had no food except what I could scrounge out of Dumpsters. It didn't take long to figure out that the ones by restaurants were bountiful with scraps. I stole food, too. When I was so hungry I couldn't stand it."

"What about the baby? Prenatal care?"

She laughed but the sound was bitter. "What part of nowhere to live and nothing to eat did you not understand? I didn't even know about prenatal care and even if I did, I couldn't take care of myself, let alone go to a doctor."

"What did you do?"

"I met a guy who took me under his wing."

Fire and ice slid into Cal's blue eyes. "A pimp?"

She nodded. "He set me up with a guy in a cheap motel, but I couldn't go through with it."

"What happened to the baby?" he asked.

Em tightened her hold on Annie as her eyes blurred with tears. "I loved that child. He was all I'd ever had that was pure and good. I couldn't stand the thought that he would be hungry and cold. That he wouldn't have a roof over his head and clothes. And toys. And a family. So I went back home, if you call a trailer park in the wrong part of town home."

"And?"

"She took me back in on the condition that I'd give the baby up for adoption." She shivered again at the cool expression in his eyes. "I went back to school, but none of the other girls were allowed to hang out with me because I was in trouble. To the boys I was fair game. After all, I couldn't get pregnant because I already was."

She'd never been so alone and lonely in her life. All she'd had was the baby growing inside her and giving him away had been like cutting out her heart and soul.

"Why didn't you tell me?" he asked.

"It's not something you just blurt out," she defended. "Hi. I'm Emily. I had a baby when I was fifteen and gave him up for adoption."

"Surely there were alternatives."

"Yeah. I chose not to say anything," she said, a bad feeling pressing on her chest.

"That's not what I meant and you know it." He stood and ran his fingers through his hair. "Did you challenge your mother's ultimatum?"

"You mean have the baby and bring him home?"

"Something like that?"

"Obviously you didn't know my mother. This was the same woman who helped me pack a bag and held the door for me when I said I'd run away if she made me give up my baby."

"I can't believe she meant that."

She couldn't believe he was missing the point. "You have supportive parents, Cal. There are a lot of kids who don't."

"What about assistance programs? State-funded agencies to help?"

"I didn't know of any and there was no one to help me find out." She took a deep breath to hold those black memories back or lose the ability to find the right words and make him understand. "I was hardly more than a child myself. I loved my child more than anything but didn't see any way to keep him. I had no alternative and it was more painful than I can tell you. That's why I'm so committed to Helping Hands and giving the girls another choice when they're in a situation like that."

He stood up and ran his fingers through his hair. "Isn't that like 'do as I say not as I do'?"

Emily stilled and couldn't get her breath. "I'm not sure I understand."

"I thought I knew you. I was wrong," he said, looking down at her.

Em stood with their daughter's solid, soundly sleeping weight in her arms. She moved to the crib and settled Annie on her back, pulling a light blanket over her bare legs and feet.

Without a word, she walked past Cal and into the living room as anger poured through her.

Moments later Cal walked in behind her. "I better go."

"I think that's a good idea," she agreed. "But first I want my say."

"Okay." He settled his hands on lean hips.

"I had no idea your sense of fairness was so impaired. You'll never know what it feels like to be a child yourself, pregnant with nowhere to turn. How dare you be so self-righteous? Until you walk in my shoes, you don't get a vote on how I lived my life."

"You should have said something."

"It was on a need-to-know basis and you didn't need to know." She stared up at him, refusing to be intimidated. Not ever again. "I came to you because the lump in my breast made me face my mortality and how that could affect Annie's future. That doesn't give you the right to pass judgment on my past. I made the best decision I could make under the circumstances. But I'm not that defenseless child any longer. We have a baby and you can always expect straightforward and honest communication where she's concerned. A child connects us, but that doesn't entitle you to run my life."

"Fair enough," he said.

After he closed the door, she sank down on the couch and refused to let the tears fall. Here he was again. Just when she'd gotten her life together. She'd thought it was safe to share with him her most personal, painful secret. She'd been wrong. But Cal was wrong about talk making her feel better.

Confession might be good for the soul, but it was hell on the heart.

Chapter Eight

Things were slow in the E.R. and this was one of the few times Cal wished he was busy, or more to the point, too busy to think about anything but helping kids. Emily claimed she had no tolerance for manipulation and lies, but at work the next day Cal was still wondering why he should believe her.

To his way of thinking, a woman with no agenda wouldn't keep information to herself. Em had done that more than once. The second time was when she found out she was pregnant with his child. The first was about her past and giving her baby up for adoption. That was important and character-defining information.

In the E.R. break room, he walked to the counter where the coffeepot sat with a stack of paper cups beside it. After grabbing one, he poured coffee into it, then sat in one of the utilitarian metal-framed chairs with orange-plastic seats. Sections of the *Review Journal* newspaper were spread out over the top of the rectangular table in the center of the room. Half-eaten bagels and donuts turning as hard as hockey pucks were scattered on top of the papers along with empty cups, napkins and an open bag of chips.

Cal moved aside the debris to find the sports section of the newspaper and opened it, but instead of baseball standings and teasers about the approaching football season, he kept seeing a pair of teasing, tempting brown eyes.

The door opened and he looked up, grateful to see Rhonda Levin standing there.

"What's up?" he asked. "Do you need me?"

The nurse manager critically scanned the table. "Easy, Doc. I just came in to straighten up this place."

"Oh."

"You sound disappointed."

"I don't know how to respond to that." He'd been hoping for something to take his mind off Emily, but that wasn't something he was prepared to say out loud. "It's like asking if you've stopped beating your wife. There's no answer that doesn't make you look bad."

"So you're bored and wanting something to do with yourself?" she asked, gathering up the trash on the table.

He knew that somewhere in the question was a deep hole just waiting for him to fall in, but wasn't quite sure where it was, making a lateral move difficult to pull off. Cautiously he said, "I was wishing to be just a little busier."

"Wow." She rolled up the top of the chip bag just a little louder than was probably necessary. "And I can't think of a single thing around here for you to give me a hand with."

"In case no one has mentioned it, sarcasm is not an attractive characteristic."

"Takes one to know one," she shot back.

"Excuse me?"

"In case no one has mentioned it to *you,* self-pity or mis-directed aggression are not especially conducive to a warm and happy work place."

"What's that supposed to mean?"

"It means that the staff has come to me with some concerns." She stacked sections of the newspaper into a pile. "You've been rude, abrasive and sarcastic to everyone today. When you're not biting someone's head off, you're brooding and looking like a man trying to decide who to take a bite out of next."

"Do you have any idea how paranoid that sounds?"

"It's not paranoia if someone is out to get you. You're in real danger of losing the Doctor-of-the-year award. The nurses, respiratory therapists and ancillary staff normally love working with you. Today—not so much. What's bugging you, Cal?" With her knuckles fisted on the table Rhonda looked down at him. "What's going on with Emily?"

It was on the tip of his tongue to blow her off, but he knew she had a point. He hadn't brought his A game to work, as far as the staff was concerned and was taking out his mood on them. Rhonda was more than the E.R. nurse manager. She was a friend.

"That day Emily showed up here in the E.R.? She came to tell me that she had my baby." He met her gaze. "Her name is Annie."

"That's old news," Rhonda informed him. "Everyone already knows."

"You're kidding. How?"

"Mitch mentioned it." She gave him a wry look. "And this is a hospital. News that interesting spreads like a virulent strain of the flu."

"Right." He knew that. And it wasn't really what bothered him. "What do you think about giving a baby away?"

"To someone on the street?" she asked wryly.

"Of course not. Adoption."

Rhonda thought for a moment. "It depends."

"On what?"

"The situation." She folded her arms over her ample chest. "You've seen abused children here in the E.R. just like I have. Under those circumstances they'd be better off with anyone besides the ones they share DNA with."

"What about an unmarried teenager?"

"Why are you asking?" She looked puzzled.

It wasn't his secret to share. As Rhonda had pointed out, this place wasn't covered by the cone of silence. "Emily is involved with a program for teenage girls who have babies on their own because their families don't support them and they have no place to go. She insists they work and get an education. In exchange reduced-cost housing is provided and the girls trade off child care. Em is their mentor."

"Good for her," Rhonda approved. "But the decision to give a baby up still depends on circumstances. Teens go from thirteen to nineteen. As far as I know they can't get a work permit until sixteen. What about the ones Emily can't help? Without assistance how can they provide diapers, food, shelter and medical care? What if they're not even old enough to drive?"

Good point.

When he didn't comment, Rhonda continued, "Kids raising kids isn't ideal. Mature adults find it a challenge, so imagine trying to raise a little life while trying to get your own started."

He'd actually faced that, then found out it was a lie. And apparently taking out the residual anger on the ones around him wasn't confined to the E.R. He'd done it to Em last night. And looking at the situation through Rhonda's eyes was giving him a different perspective. "So you think teen mothers should give up their children?"

"Don't put words in my mouth," she warned. "The issue isn't black and white. It's not neat and tidy. Every woman is going to have a different take on the decision. But let me just say that I have a great respect for women who put their baby's welfare above their own needs."

"What do you mean?" he asked.

"It's an incredibly courageous decision and a different slant on unselfish love. Imagine a young woman who isn't in a place where she can give her baby all the opportunities she might wish. Somehow she finds the strength to relinquish her child to two loving parents who are unable to conceive a baby."

He looked at her face and saw the traces of pain lingering in the tight mouth and shadowed eyes. "What, Rhonda?"

She blinked and tried to smile, but couldn't quite pull it off. "I couldn't get pregnant."

"You wanted kids?"

"Very much," she said softly. "My husband wasn't in favor of adoption. He said the two of us together were good and more than enough for him. We made it work. We're still together and very happy."

"Good for you."

"The point is that giving a child up shouldn't be looked at in a negative way. It's a chance for that baby to have a shot at a really good life and every innocent baby deserves that." She rubbed a finger beneath her nose. "Listen to me on my soapbox. I guess you could say I've got a soft spot for the little ones."

"Yeah."

"Bet you're sorry you got me started." A puzzled look settled on her face. "But your baby wasn't given away. She's with her mom. You know about her. So, mind if I ask why you wanted to know my feelings about adoption?"

"Just curious." Again, not his secret to spread around.

"Emily told you about your daughter. Better late than never. For the record, I'm giving her the benefit of the doubt because I know her. She's one of the good ones."

"You're not the first one to mention that."

And Annie wasn't her first pregnancy but this time she'd been in a position to take care of herself and the baby. Points to her for that.

"Look, Cal, this is just my opinion and worth what you paid for it. But—"

"What?" Since his doctor-of-the-year award was on the line he didn't say what was on the tip of his tongue.

"You're not getting any younger. Unlike the women you've been dating recently. And I use the term *women* in the loosest possible way."

"What does that mean?"

"Don't play dumb with me. We both know it means that by going out with women barely of legal age you're weeding out a mature woman who's going to want a commitment."

"The women I see *are* less demanding. It works for me. I couldn't be more content with my social life." It was Emily who disturbed him.

"You're spitting into the wind, if you ask me."

"And by that you mean?"

"If you keep creating obstacles where none exist, you're going to wind up a crabby and lonely old man." She walked to the door and opened it, then turned back for one last shot. "My husband and I couldn't have children, but we've gotten past it and have a good, fulfilling life. If you don't make peace with whatever it is that's holding you back yours will not be pretty."

It already wasn't pretty.

He'd become attached to a child that *never* existed because he'd been lied to. Emily was the only woman he'd ever regretted losing, until learning she'd also lied. He'd be there for his daughter. And he'd be there for Emily insofar as it concerned their daughter. If loneliness was the price he paid, he could live with that.

He'd learned the hard way that being alone was far better than being with someone who made you miserable with lies. Emily was the second woman to make a sucker out of him and no one would get another shot.

Not even her.

Sometimes being right was hell, Emily thought, navigating the streets to Cal's house on Saturday. Every instinct had told her he would never understand why she'd given up her baby, not even if that baby went to a loving home that she'd been unable to provide. Unfortunately he hadn't disappointed her.

He thought she was a horrible person. Maybe that was just as well. If she couldn't put the brakes on her feelings, Cal's low opinion of her character would do the job just fine.

She hadn't seen him since that night earlier in the week. One minute he'd loved her and the next he couldn't stand the sight of her. This swimming date with their daughter was the last thing she wanted to do, but she'd given her word. Eventually Annie would be comfortable with him and wouldn't require Em to be around, but today wasn't that day. Today she had to pretend she didn't care what he thought.

Sex with Cal had been a mistake, but that didn't stop her from wanting him again.

She steered her car into the driveway and turned it off, then noticed Cal peeking through the living room shutter. God help me, she thought, wishing it was indifference coursing through her instead of anticipation.

"Rome wasn't built in a day," she muttered to herself, exiting the car, then opening the back passenger door. "It will be easier now that I know the score."

He walked out the front door. "Hi."

Em heard his voice as she reached into the backseat for Annie. "Sorry I'm late."

"No big deal."

Yeah, right.

"It was just one of those days when nothing went as planned." She unhooked Annie from the car seat. "Annie's nap was longer than usual and I didn't want to wake her too soon. That would make her crabby for the afternoon and no one would have a good time."

She straightened with Annie, who sleepily rested her head on Em's shoulder. Putting nerves aside, she glanced up at Cal, fully expecting the cold expression that had chilled her to the core just a few days before. Em was surprised to see him not looking that way at all.

"What?" she asked suspiciously.

"What, what?" he shot back.

"You're smiling."

"I'm happy to see you guys."

Ah. Because he hadn't trusted her to show up at all. "I said I'd bring her for a swim."

"Yes, you did." Frowning, he folded his arms over his wide chest. "Em, about that night at your apartment. I want to—"

"It was a moment of weakness." She so didn't want to talk about that night. If only it was a paragraph on the computer that she could delete, effectively erasing the erotic scene from her memory. And heaven forbid he think she was that easy or vulnerable to him. "The thing is, I'd have been susceptible to any man. It's been a long time for me."

"So any man would do?"

The words were teasing and should have made her feel better but fell short of that mark. "You were handy. That's all."

"I see."

"Don't be offended. I'm just saying. Straightforward and honest." She shrugged.

"Good to know."

She was tempted to tell him that there wouldn't be any more moments of weakness but decided against it because she'd assured him she didn't lie.

"Actually, that's not what I wanted to talk about," he said.

What else could there possibly be? she wondered. But in the spirit of cooperation it seemed wrong to shut him down.

"Oh?" she asked, hoping it wasn't an invitation to more emotional damage.

"About the way I behaved after—"

Heat rose to her cheeks that had nothing to do with the hot sun and she reached into the backseat to hide the reaction. The highlights of their last time together had been sex and him being a jerk, making it an impressively bad evening in every possible way. "Forget it."

"Can't." He ran his fingers through his hair. "I acted like an ass."

She straightened and met his gaze. He looked completely serious. "Did you just say you were an ass?"

"I did."

"Just checking." That admission from Cal Westen made her wonder if there wasn't hope for world peace. "I needed to confirm before saying you'll get no argument from me."

"Thanks for making this apology easier," he said wryly. "I appreciate your compassion."

"What goes around comes around." He hadn't made her painful confession of past mistakes easy and needed to know how she felt. She was a grown woman, not a defenseless teen who craved his goodwill, no matter that she wanted it. Getting over him would take time, but she'd handle that, too.

"I behaved badly."

She blinked again. More words that took her aback. "Yes, you did."

"I apologize."

There wasn't a cloud in the sky, but she expected lightning to strike her any second. She couldn't believe what she was hearing. "Who are you and what have you done with Cal?"

When Annie lifted her head, he held out his arms and she went to him. "Rhonda gave me a different perspective on the issue." He must have detected something in her expression because he added, "I didn't share your story. We were talking in general terms. But I had no right to judge. You were right about that and I won't do it again."

"If you say so."

"I'll do my best."

Cal nuzzled his daughter's neck, and Em liked hearing her giggle. It lightened the mood and dispelled the tension between them even though that left little in the way of cover for her to hide behind.

She followed him into the family room and set the diaper bag on the coffee table.

"Her swimsuit is on under the sundress," she told him.

"Are you going in the pool with us?" he asked.

"Yeah." Except now she wished she had her one-piece tank suit on underneath her shorts and T-shirt instead of the bikini. That had been an act of vengeance and now she knew what they meant about revenge being a double-edged sword. At the time she'd never expected Cal to admit he was wrong.

"Okay."

Annie squirmed in his arms, which he obviously knew meant she wanted down because he set her on her feet and managed to slide her dress off before she moved out of reach. When she went for the entertainment center and reached for the electrical cords, he moved quickly, showing his improving protective instincts.

"That's probably not a good idea," he said grabbing her up. When she let out a screech of frustration, he said, "Sorry, little bit. Electricity is not kid-friendly."

Em used the distraction to slide out of her shorts and T-shirt, hoping not to draw his attention. "Good work, slick. You're developing some impressive skills with our daughter."

He couldn't quite hide his once-over of her from head to toe and something like appreciation glittered in his eyes. "Thanks. I simply executed a flanking maneuver that saved her from herself."

"TV cords are a constant source of curiosity," she said.

"I see she's done this before."

"Every chance she gets." She realized they were commiserating as parents. Bonding. That was a potential source of trouble. "Baby proofing helps, but there's no way to remove every single temptation. And I'm not so sure that would be good. She needs to learn there are some things that just can't be touched."

When Cal whipped off his own T-shirt she knew she was looking at one of them right now. He was naked except for swim trunks. His wide, tanned shoulders and broad chest tapered to a flat abdomen dusted with a masculine sprinkling of hair that made her fingers itch to touch. But if *he* touched *her* she'd get burned like before. Avoidance therapy was successful for a baby, but apparently not for her. She still wanted him, in spite of the way he'd reacted to her confession. In spite of knowing he was a commitment-phobe, with the exception of his daughter.

"Are you ready to go swimming?" he said to Annie.

"She needs sunscreen on first." Em pulled the tube out of the diaper bag and took the little girl from him, grazing his warm skin with her fingers.

"You've got a pretty impressive skill set yourself," he marveled. "Hanging on to a slippery toddler can't be easy."

"Practice," she said, finishing up with the cream. Today was all about practicing to resist him. "Do you need sunscreen?"

The words were out before she realized that would be flirting with danger.

"Yeah. Thanks." He turned his back to her.

She squeezed a large blob into her hand, then smoothed it over his broad, smooth shoulders and the muscles of his back. Touching his warm skin made her shiver, then go hot all over and she forced herself to concentrate, to make sure every inch of flesh was protected from the sun's harmful rays. Exposure to Cal was not new, but now he represented a different kind of harm.

"Your turn," he said, taking the tube from her. He moved his index finger in a circle indicating she should turn her back.

She did, but not looking at him was only marginally less potent than staring into his sexy blue eyes. Then she felt his big, strong hands rubbing the cream on her neck, shoulders and lower back. He lifted the strings of her bikini top to make sure she was covered and the intimate touch made her shiver again.

"Cold?" he asked, a smile in his voice.

"Yeah. You know me and the air-conditioning."

"I remember." He finished as fast as possible and backed away. "Ready?"

"Hmm?" she asked, glancing over her shoulder.

"To go swimming. Last one in is a rotten egg."

He grabbed up Annie and walked outside, then stepped with her into the shallow end of the pool. Annie slapped the surface of the water with a chubby hand and laughed when she splashed herself. He glanced over when Em closed the slider behind her. The sunglasses over his eyes protected them, but also her from the hungry expression she thought she'd just seen in them.

Emily sat on the side of the pool and dangled her feet in the water. "We need to give Annie swim lessons. There are programs for kids her age that teach them to be water safe. If she's going to spend time with you here, it would be a good idea."

He stared at her. "You'd be willing to leave Annie here with me?"

"Of course. You're her father."

"I know. But—" He shook his head as a pleased smile turned up the corners of his mouth. "What an awesome responsibility."

"I thought it's what you wanted."

"I do. It's a great idea. I'd be happy to watch her when you have to work. And not because I don't trust that you leave her in a safe place."

"I know what you mean. And since we both have jobs, juggling child care would be helpful," she finished lamely.

He settled Annie more securely on his strong forearm. "And you're right about swim lessons. In the E.R. I've seen way too many pool accidents with kids." He hugged the little girl until she squealed to lean over and splash the water. "I don't ever want to have to say 'if only' because we didn't do something we should have."

"You're right."

Em was very relieved that she wasn't in this parenting thing on her own. Partly because when she looked back at her own life, the "if onlys" piled up like a multicar freeway accident.

If only she'd made better decisions when she was a teenager. If only she'd told Cal about the pregnancy instead of reading his feelings into the words he'd said. Show don't tell. Everything he'd shown since finding out about his daughter showed her that he'd commit when his heart was in it. If only his heart was into her, Em thought sadly.

She watched him laugh with Annie and felt something tighten in her chest. He'd admitted he was wrong to judge her and that made her like him more. He was a good dad and a decent person. She'd loved loving him but it couldn't happen again. If she'd never kept the truth from him, maybe. But she had.

He would never forgive her for that.

Chapter Nine

Cal peeked into Emily's bedroom to see if she and Annie were finally asleep.

"Affirmative," he whispered to himself as he pulled the door almost closed. He left it cracked so he could hear if they needed anything.

That morning he'd driven Em to the outpatient surgery center at Mercy Medical Center for removal of the breast lump. Her ultrasound had been inconclusive and the doctor decided getting it out was the best treatment option. He concurred.

So he'd waited with Annie in the waiting room while her mom went through the procedure. Stress in body and mind had sapped Em's energy, although she'd put up impressive resistance when he'd suggested she rest. Not even pulling medical rank on her had worked. What finally convinced her was settling Annie.

Their little girl had a tough day with her dad. She'd hung

in there with him until reaching a point when only Mom would do. Then Em had to be careful because of her stitches. Annie knew something was off and reacted by voicing at a decibel level only auditory to dogs that she was *not* napping by herself in her crib. So Em rested on the bed with her and now the two were sound asleep.

He looked around the living room wondering what to do with himself while he stood guard over them. Leaving wasn't an option until he knew Em wouldn't have a problem handling a one-year-old while recovering from her procedure. It crossed his mind that it might be just an excuse to stay, but he immediately dismissed that thought. If his daughter needed him he'd be there for her.

A knock on the door sounded as loud as a gunshot, and he hurried to see who was there. He opened up and saw Patty on the sidewalk with towheaded Henry in her arms.

"Hi, Dr. Westen."

"Hey." He stepped outside and pulled the front door almost closed behind him. A young guy was on the sidewalk in front of her apartment working on a child-size table.

She noticed where he was looking and said, "That's Jonas Blackford, Henry's father."

"Okay."

"I told him about you, how you checked out Henry when he was sick."

Cal looked at the little guy in her arms who stopped squirming to get down long enough to look back at him. Henry was the picture of health now. "How's he doing?"

"Perfect," Patty said, lovingly brushing a hand over the boy's white-blond hair. "But that's not why I came over."

"Oh?"

"How's Em?" She looked worried. "She told Lucy and I that the breast lump was being removed today. We wanted to be there, but with work and the kids… Anyway, she said you were driving her and watching Annie."

"That's right."

"So how is she? Can I see her?"

"She's sleeping right now," he answered. That didn't remove the worried look from the teen's face. "Only because going through the procedure took a lot out of her. She's fine."

"Really? Was it cancer?"

"The surgeon doesn't think so."

"Is there any way to be sure?" she asked doubtfully. "Her mom died of breast cancer."

That surprised him. She hadn't shared that there was a family history of breast cancer. More secrets?

"The mass is being biopsied," he explained. "I've called in some favors at Mercy Medical Center. The lab is going to expedite the test results and call me."

He'd been expecting the call for a while now but didn't mention that to the teen.

"Will you let me know when you hear?" Patty asked. "Lucy and I are concerned."

"No problem," he said.

She half turned. "Come meet Jonas."

There was no good reason to decline so he said, "Okay."

Patty turned and walked over to the young man bent over the small table. "Babe?"

He straightened and smiled at the little boy who grinned at him. "Hey, dude."

"I want you to meet Dr. Westen," Patty said. "Remember, I told you about him?"

"Yeah." He looked up and held out his hand. "Jonas Blackford."

"Nice to meet you." They shook hands and the kid had a firm grip. "Cal Westen. That's a good-looking boy you've got there."

"He looks just like his daddy," Patty said proudly.

"I can see that." Cal studied them. Jonas was shorter than himself, but muscular and compact. His hair was a darker blond than his son's, but the angular structure of their faces was identical, as was the blue eye color. Henry was going to be a chick magnet when he grew up. "What are you working on there?"

Jonas glanced down. "A table for Henry."

"And Oscar when he's a little bigger."

Cal squatted and ran a hand over the smooth wood top and sturdy legs. "Nice job."

"Thanks." Jonas smiled. "It's just about ready for stain."

"But that's going to have to wait for next payday," Patty shared.

Cal remembered strict budgeting way back when, along with tension and a feeling of waiting for the other shoe to drop. It seemed like a long time ago, but that was because he did his best to forget the drama, trauma and bitterness. He didn't get the feeling that these two were anything but poor and happy.

"Uh-oh." Patty sniffed her son, then peeked in the back of his denim shorts. "Someone needs a change."

"Don't look at me," Jonas teased.

Patty laughed. "It's your turn."

They joked back and forth until Jonas finally said, "Seriously, I'll change him if you want."

"That's okay. I can do it. You're almost finished and I don't want to interrupt." Patty kissed his cheek, then disappeared through the apartment's front door.

Cal looked at Jonas, trying to think of something to make conversation with a kid he had little in common with. "So how's it going?"

"You know. Working full-time keeps me busy." The teen brushed his forearm across his forehead. "I've got a break between summer classes and the fall semester, but it feels like a vacation. I get to spend more time with Patty and Henry."

"Where do you work?"

"At the Suncoast Hotel. I park cars but I'm off today."

"I hear that can be pretty good money."

Jonas shrugged. "Can't complain."

"What are you studying in school?"

"Accounting."

"Are your grades good?" Cal asked.

"You sound like my dad." He shrugged again. "They're not bad."

Cal wanted to ask how he kept up the grind, but he already knew. At the same age, he'd only juggled school and work because the baby part had been a lie. His own grades had gone up because he'd used studying as an excuse to get away every time his wife had pulled some episode for attention, a half-hearted pill overdose or wrist wound. After every stunt, he'd put a bandage on the relationship, then bury himself in classes, internship or residency and shoot to the top of the class.

His folks had taught him not to take marriage vows lightly and he'd stayed because it was the right thing to do. But Patty and Jonas hadn't taken vows and he wondered what was keeping them together.

"So you like spending time with Patty and the little guy?" Cal asked.

Jonas met his gaze. "Yeah."

No elaboration. "If you're here all the time anyway, why not get married?"

"Because my folks are helping, and I want to wait until I can take care of Patty and Henry by myself. Both of us need an education so we can make a life for Henry. Just because we're not married doesn't mean I won't be there for them."

Cal remembered what Em had said about education. She

was right and the teens were definitely taking her philosophy to heart. His respect for her wisdom and courage continued to grow.

Patty came back outside with Henry who was carrying a toy car. When he saw Cal, he dropped it and held out his arms.

"Hey, big guy," Cal said. "I take it operation diaper change was successful?"

"Oh, yeah," Patty said. "He's a happy camper now."

"Where's Lucy?" Cal asked.

She and Jonas exchanged a glance before Patty answered. "Her boyfriend showed up a couple of weeks ago."

"Oscar's dad?"

Jonas nodded. "He *says* he wants to be around."

"You don't sound convinced." Cal settled Henry on his forearm.

"For Lucy's sake I hope he's sincere," Patty said. "But it seems to me that if he'd wanted to support her, he'd have been around when she was pregnant and Oscar was born."

"Maybe he had a good reason," Cal suggested, being that he hadn't known about Annie.

Before they could answer, the door behind him opened and Emily walked out with Annie in her arms. Cal's first thought was that she shouldn't be doing any lifting, but before he could say so, Annie took one look at him holding Henry and started to fuss and hold out her arms.

"She wants you to take her," Em pointed out.

"Imagine that." He gave Henry to Jonas and took his daughter. "If I'd only known that jealousy was the way to win her heart."

Like father, like daughter. Cal had last felt the sting of the green-eyed monster while watching his partner hug Em. That shouldn't have bothered him but it did, although he refused to believe it was because he wanted her for himself. He wouldn't be that stupid again.

"How do you feel?" he asked Em.

"Not too bad." She rolled her shoulder. "A little sore. I'm just glad it's over."

"Me, too."

The four of them chatted for a while, letting the children play and toddle outside. Jonas gave Henry a small piece of sandpaper and tried to show him how to smooth out the top of the table. But when he and Annie kept sticking it in their mouths, it was agreed that handyman skills would have to come a little later.

When Cal's cell phone rang, everyone's attention turned on him. "Yeah," he answered.

"Cal, it's Dennis from the lab."

"What have you got for me?"

"The biopsy for Emily Summers that you wanted. It's benign. No evidence of abnormal cells. Just your garden-variety intraductal papilloma."

Relief flooded through him. "Good to hear. Thanks, Dennis."

"No problem."

He flipped his phone closed and looked at the three expectant faces. "It's benign."

"Thank goodness," Patty said to Em. "I'd hug you but I'm afraid I'd hurt you."

Cal's sentiments exactly. "This is cause for celebration."

"What did you have in mind?" Em looked as relieved as he felt.

"Barbecue. Your place. I'll get the hamburgers, hot dogs and everything else." He looked at the teens. "You guys are invited. And Henry."

"Cool," Jonas said.

On the way to his car, Cal glanced over his shoulder to look at Emily. She was smiling with the teens and helping keep the two toddlers out of mischief. The motley group was her family, he realized. Iy choice. The relatives she'd picked for herself. He'd always had his parents and brother, but their family dynamic was different. It was subtle but understood that you handled your problems because that was the right thing to do.

And that's why he'd married his girlfriend when she claimed to be pregnant. Instead of a helpmate, she'd been another kind of problem and he'd done his best to handle it.

Emily helped the teens because she understood their problems and empathized. They needed her. Cal had gotten used to not needing anyone, but prolonged exposure to Emily was changing that. And he had to do something to stop it. Now that her health crisis was resolved, he could just be Annie's dad, and only her dad, because Annie's mom could rip his heart out.

A little after five in the afternoon Emily drove into the parking lot at Nooks and Nannies, The Nanny Network Child Care Center nestled between Maryland Parkway, Tropicana Avenue, Flamingo and Paradise Roads, not far from McCarran International Airport. She pulled into an empty space close to the entrance. The one-story white-stucco building had a red-tile roof and fenced in yard with equipment that included swings, a sand box, climbing apparatus and a playhouse.

The facility had an excellent reputation as well as impressive adult-to-child ratios that ensured a safe environment. As if that wasn't enough plusses, her best friend, Sophia Green, worked here. She remembered telling Cal that Sophia had been there for her when Annie was born. She'd left out of her narrative the parts after the birth when Sophia supported her through the next six months of maternal confidence crisis. Her friend had been the voice of reason during hormonal fluctuations, sleep deprivation and everything in between.

Although she knew it was the right decision to tell Cal

about their daughter, she also had Sophia to thank for the current emotional upheaval telling him had caused. Absently she touched her fingertips to her chest, grateful the lump was gone and had turned out not to be serious. The same couldn't be said for her situation with Cal.

Em got out of the car and locked it, then walked to the dark double-glass entrance doors and pulled open the one on the right. A blast of cold air hit her and it felt good after the August heat outside. This building housed administration offices and separate rooms for meetings, Mommy and Me classes and community education workshops.

She turned right into the first office reception area noting that there was no one behind the desk. Probably the receptionist was gone for the day. Em tapped lightly on the half-open door and Sophia glanced up from her computer monitor.

Sophia had a beautiful smile but her gray eyes never quite lost their tinge of sadness. A byproduct of doing social work for the Clark County Child-Welfare Department. She'd intervened for kids who needed help most and could break your heart with their stories. The children she'd helped were grateful. The ones she couldn't haunted her and that's what had influenced her decision to work in the private sector.

Sophia's reddish-brown hair cut in a short, shiny bob enhanced her girl-next-door prettiness. Men wanted her; women envied her. Em loved her loyalty and friendship.

She lifted a hand in greeting. "Hi."

Sophia got up and came around the desk for a hug. "Hi, yourself. You're here to pick up Annie?"

"Yeah." Because Cal was working and couldn't watch her.

"It's been a while since you stopped in to see me."

"I know. I'm usually in a hurry when I come by. Things have been crazy since—"

Glancing away from her friend's direct look, Em studied

the pictures on the walls. The black-and-white photographs were enlarged and framed, arranged in groupings. There were no people in them, just outdoor scenes—ocean, lake, mountains and forests. This wasn't the first time she'd noticed them, but it occurred to her that in a world where nothing was ever black and white, at least it could be that way in Sophia's space.

She leaned a hip on the corner of her desk and finished the thought about why things had been crazy. "Since you told Cal he has a daughter?"

"Pretty much."

"How's that going?"

"Oh, you know." Em shrugged.

"If I knew, I wouldn't have asked. What don't you want to talk about?"

"So many things, so little time."

Sophia nodded. "Okay. Why don't you start with Cal. How is he?"

Handsome. Charismatic. Sexy.

"He's fine."

"What does he think of his daughter?"

Em smiled at the instant mental image of Cal playing with Annie in the pool. He was playful, protective and positively awesome. "I guess I'd have to say that he's pretty much in love with his little girl."

"That doesn't surprise me," Sophia said.

"It surprises me after all the things he said about commitment being a four-letter word. I honestly figured he would say thanks, but no thanks and that would be the extent of our interaction."

"But since you're now too busy to stop by and say hello when you pick up Annie, I'd have to assume that he's at least marginally involved in your life."

"You could say that," Em hedged.

"Care to elaborate?"

Did she have to? But Em knew any attempt to dodge the question would be a waste of time.

"Cal has embraced fatherhood enthusiastically. He's learning about his daughter. He was there for me when I saw the doctor—"

"Oh, my gosh, I can't believe I forgot to ask." Sophia shook her head. "What did the doctor say?"

"I had tests and finally had the lump removed. It was an intraductal papilloma—"

"English please."

"A small wartlike growth in a milk duct. Completely harmless."

"Thank goodness," Sophia said. "Remind me to punish you severely for not letting me know."

"Considering the fact that I'm dealing with Caleb Westen fallout, I would ask you to cut me some slack."

"Done," her friend agreed. "But it's a one-time pass, and I'd advise you not to let it happen again."

"I swear." Em made a cross over her heart to seal the promise.

"Okay, then. So tell me about the fallout. What's going on?"

Em sank into one of the visitor chairs. "He's doing all the right things. Offered financial support."

"Knowing and loving you as I do, I'm guessing it was refused?"

"Yeah. He didn't believe at first that I wasn't after money. Or something."

"Or something?" Sophia crossed her arms over her chest. "If he's the picture of paternal perfection, why don't you look happier?"

"For starters, he doesn't trust me. After not telling him about Annie, I can't say I blame him."

"But? And I know there is one."

"You and I know that everyone has reason to question their faith in people to varying degrees. We've all been let down at one time or another. But, Soph, it goes deeper with Cal."

"How do you know?"

Em thought about how to put this into words. "It's a feeling really. The way he questions everything. And—"

"What?" her friend prompted.

"Something his father said." She smiled softly. "It was Annie's first birthday. A party at his house."

"I wasn't invited."

"I'll make it up to you." Em sighed. "It's no excuse, but I've had a lot on my plate. I realize now how selfish it was to keep Cal in the dark about Annie. His folks met her for the first time on her birthday. They adored her on sight and barely managed to keep in check their hostility toward me. Again, I don't blame them. But his father said something."

"Which was?"

"About Cal's past. When I asked him to cut me some slack—" Em smiled wryly. "Apparently I'm doing that to everyone lately."

"You think?"

Ignoring the barb, she continued, "Anyway, I was explaining that I had my reasons for keeping quiet about the pregnancy but didn't want to talk about them. His dad said I wasn't the only one with baggage. Cal was married."

Sophia frowned. "Did you get the details?"

"He said it was Cal's story to tell."

"Can't argue with that, Em. And you won't have to ask. Cal will tell you if he wants you to know."

Emily twisted her fingers together in her lap. "Something happened to him."

"That doesn't make him unique," Sophia said. "It's not your problem, Em. What do you care what he thinks of you?"

"I don't. Not really. Except that his opinion could impact Annie's perceptions."

"That's not what's getting to you. It's more personal." Sophia tapped her index finger against her lips. "You're falling for him again, aren't you?"

"Don't be silly," Em scoffed. "I'm smarter than that. *Again* implies I had deep feelings the first time around, but I walked away, remember?"

"Not without regret." Her friend's eyes narrowed suspiciously. "You slept with him, didn't you?"

Technically when he'd had his way with her they were standing up and no one had been sleeping, least of all her. Em shivered with the memory of how desperately she'd wanted him. "Why would you think that?"

"Oh, please. Don't even try to wiggle your way out of telling me. You're a very bad liar."

"Cal wouldn't agree with you about that. And the truth is that we *were* intimate." Em squirmed in the chair. "Please don't lecture me. Anything you say is nothing compared to what I've said to myself. It was stupid and won't happen again."

"Because you got him out of your system?"

If only. From her mouth to God's ear.

"I'm still working on it. The problem is now that he knows about Annie and has taken to being a father, there won't be any way not to see him."

"So what you're saying is that the only way you can get over him is out of sight, out of mind?"

It was more like out of the frying pan into the fire. Em didn't want to admit that not seeing Cal hadn't worked very well in getting over him.

"Look, Soph, I'm sailing in uncharted waters here. I didn't mean to keep you out of the loop."

"I know. That's not your style, and no one knows that

better than me. But it's too much fun and too easy to give you a hard time."

Em grinned. "I'll get even with you. Don't think I won't—" Her cell phone range interrupting her. She dug it out of her purse and flipped it open. "Hello?"

"Em? It's Patty."

She knew from the teen's tone that something was wrong. "What is it?"

"Henry fell and hit his head. He's bleeding. He's not crying—like he's out of it. Jonas wants to take him to the clinic, but I don't think that's best—"

"Go to Mercy Medical Center, Patty," she said. "Cal's there. He'll take care of Henry."

"What if he won't?" There was panic in Patty's voice.

"He will because I'm going to call him right now. I'll meet you at the E.R." Just in case they needed backup. She flipped her phone closed and looked at her friend. "Can you keep Annie for me?"

"Of course. I'll bring Annie home with me. Sounds like Patty needs you more right now."

"Thanks. I'll get her as soon as I can. I owe you more than I can say, but right now I have to go."

Chapter Ten

Emily parked her car outside Mercy Medical Center's emergency entrance and hurried into the crowded waiting area. She scanned the faces and didn't see Patty and Jonas, which meant either that they'd been taken to an exam room or hadn't arrived yet. Stopping at the information desk, she was just about to ask which when Cal came through the double doors to meet her.

Without a word he took her elbow and guided her to a quiet place in the hall just around the corner. She'd felt so scared and alone during the twenty-minute drive here that his hand on her arm felt really good. It was warm and safe, a sensation that had never been very familiar to her until Cal. And she didn't want to count on it—especially from Cal.

"Hi," she said, meeting his gaze. "Did Patty and Jonas get here yet?"

He nodded. "After you called me I was waiting for them."

"How's Henry? Can I see him?" She tried to read his expression, wondering if he was worried or just tired. "I know I'm not family. Technically. But Patty wants me to be there for her."

"Henry's not back there."

"Where is he?"

"Having tests." He ran his fingers through his hair. "CAT scan and EEG."

Her stomach knotted. "Is it more than just a bump on the head? Patty said he was bleeding."

"There can be a lot of blood from a head wound, which doesn't necessarily mean severe trauma. But—"

"I hate that word!" she said fiercely. "Why is he having tests?"

"To rule out bleeding in the brain that can cause intracranial pressure. He's lethargic. Could be a slight concussion. Not severe," he assured her when she sucked in a breath. "He didn't lose consciousness, but—"

She stared at him. "There's that word again."

"Let's just say he's not the same energetic kid who wore me out at the barbecue. I just want to be sure."

"Did they tell you what happened?"

"He was running and tripped over a toy. Hit his head on a table. The one Jonas was making for him," he added.

"Oh, no." Her heart twisted.

"For sure he's going to need stitches to close the laceration," he said.

"How are Patty and Jonas holding up?"

"They're putting on a brave front to keep Henry calm. But you can see the fear in their eyes, like every concerned parent with a child in the E.R."

There was something in his eyes that she'd never seen before. After dating for a while she'd gotten to know him pretty well but this expression was new. "It's different for you now, isn't it?"

"Care to be more specific?"

She tilted her head to the side and studied him intently. "You understand how the moms and dads feel when their children are suffering," she observed.

"How did you know?"

"Because of Annie." She was talking more about herself when she added, "When you're walking in the same shoes it's hard to ignore the pain because you know what they're going through."

And because of the baby she'd given up, she understood so many more things. She knew Patty and Jonas were struggling to do right by their little boy because they'd made the decision to raise him against their families' advice and didn't want to hear the I-told-you-so. But it was more than that. Again she understood because of the baby she gave away and Annie. The love for their little boy was bigger and more consuming than anything else. Giving him a perfect, pain-free life was their only goal, however impossible.

"Doctor Westen?"

They glanced at the young woman in scrubs standing by one of the open double doors separating them from the trauma bays.

"What is it, Gretchen?"

"The Blackford boy is back from radiology."

"Thanks. Tell his parents I'll be right in."

"Yes, Doctor."

Emily looked up at him. "That was fast."

He shrugged. "I pulled some strings."

"So Henry took cuts?"

"Maybe." A small smile threatened at the corners of his mouth. "But no one's medical care was compromised."

"How long will it take to get the results?" Em asked.

"Guaranteed in thirty minutes. I'm going to call right now and see if I can't get them sooner," he answered. "Do you want to see Patty?"

"Yeah."

To avoid the crowded waiting area he led her through the maze of halls, which was the back way into the trauma bays. He walked past curtained areas that protected the privacy of patients being tended to and dodged various mysterious machines with dials and tubes and equipment carts. They were on wheels to make them portable but for the time being had served their purpose and were hastily parked until needed again. He indicated the third room on the right.

"Stay with them. I'll be back as soon as I can."

"Okay."

Em watched his broad shoulders until he turned a corner and disappeared. She felt the loss of his warmth and security. She spent time here and worked with patients after Cal had saved their lives or did what he did to get them back on the road to health. But tonight it felt like she was making her way through a foreign country because a little boy she cared very much about was hurt. Thank goodness Cal was here.

She walked into the room where the young mother sat on the bed holding Henry. Her sleeveless white T-shirt had brownish stains that were no doubt her baby's dried blood. Jonas stood beside the two of them looking angry, which meant he was feeling worried and helpless.

Then Patty saw her and a tear slid from the corner of her eye. "Emily—"

Em rushed over to them and gave the teen a quick hug. "Hi, kiddo. How is he?"

"Not having a good day," Patty said.

She sat beside the young mom and gently rubbed a hand on the toddler's chubby leg. A gauze square covered the gash on his forehead and he was unusually quiet. "Hi, Henry. Did you get an owie?"

"Big time," Jonas said.

"Cal is checking on the test results now. I'm sure he'll have some news soon."

"He'll need stitches," Patty said, looking scared at the prospect.

"We wish he didn't have to go through that," Em said. "But I can't think of anyone I'd rather have take care of him than Cal. Henry is in very good hands."

He loved his job and was very good at it. That's one of the things that had attracted her from the very beginning and why she'd advised Patty to bring her little boy here to Cal.

He walked into the room and they all looked at him expectantly. "The tests came out fine," he said, not wasting time. "Good thing Henry has such a hard head."

"Thank goodness." Patty reached a hand up to Jonas who instantly squeezed it.

"All the news is positive, but to be on the safe side I'd like to admit Henry and keep him overnight for observation—"

Patty glanced worriedly at Jonas. "Can't we watch him at home? You could tell us what to look for."

Cal rubbed a hand over his neck. "This is about not having medical insurance, right?"

"Yeah." Jonas brushed a gentle hand over his son's matted hair. "Don't get me wrong, Doc. I want him to have what he needs. But I'm not sure how I'm going to pay for everything already."

"It's not as bad as you think," Cal said.

"That's because you're not the one on the hook for it." Jonas crossed his arms over his chest. "Everything always costs more than you think."

"I don't recommend taking him home yet."

Henry sat up and pointed at Cal. "Cookie?"

"Hey, you. Feeling better, big guy?" Patty looked at him. "But he's perked up, almost back to normal."

Cal blew out a long breath. "It may not be necessary, but I'd rather err on the side of caution."

Jonas shifted from one foot to the other. "Look, man, Patty and I appreciate everything you've done. And we respect your opinion. But we'll watch out for him ourselves."

"Then you'll be taking him home AMA." He saw their confused looks and added, "Against medical advice."

Emily knew the intense expression on Cal's face and had been on the receiving end quite a bit lately. She also knew it was generated because he sincerely cared. Both sides had a point and she watched from the cheap seats between a rock and a hard place.

"There must be some kind of compromise between caution and common sense," Emily said. "If he's at home there are four adults to take turns looking out for him and you can tell us what to watch for."

"Like a family," Cal said.

"That's what we are." She wondered why he was staring at her as if she'd come from another planet. "And just so we're clear, I've got your cell number if we have any questions."

"I'll go you one better." He glanced at the watch on his wrist. "How about this. My shift is almost over. You guys hang here until then, and I'll come home with you and stay the night, to direct the troops."

Patty and Jonas exchanged a look, before she said, "Why?"

Cal met her gaze. "Because Henry is my daughter's best friend."

That was guy speak for how much he cared and Emily's heart did a stop, drop and roll maneuver that was completely involuntary.

"You don't have to, man." Jonas sounded as if he wasn't accustomed to catching a break.

"It's what I do." He looked at her. "My compromise. Take

it or leave it. And before answering you should know that I'll be there no matter what you say. And I know where you live."

Emily cleared the lump from her throat before saying, "As far as the rest of the cost for Henry's E.R. visit, I'll look into finding a way to pay for everything. It's what *I* do. I'll talk to Sister Monica. This is a nonprofit hospital and they have to give back a certain amount to the community to maintain their tax-exempt status."

"My medical group bills independently from the hospital and I'll write off my time," Cal offered.

Patty blinked up at him. "We don't want charity."

"The heck we don't," Jonas argued.

Cal grinned. "Attaboy."

"Jonas, I thought we agreed we were going to do this on our own," Patty said.

"You are," Cal assured her. "But give people a chance to lend a hand. It makes us feel good about ourselves."

"You're just saying that so we won't feel bad," she accused, as Henry started squirming in her lap.

"Is it working?" he asked.

"I'm good, man." Jonas took his son when the boy held out his arms.

"His male pride is off life support, that just leaves your maternal instincts." Cal looked from one parent to the other. "Let me help. Just because I can."

"But coming with us to watch Henry is enough," Patty protested. "We can't ask you to donate more of your time."

"Technically, you didn't ask. I volunteered. So it's settled." He nodded with satisfaction. "Now I'll just get my little buddy stitched up. Don't worry. I'll make him as comfortable as possible."

When he left the room to get what he needed for the repair, Emily followed. "Cal?"

He turned. "Hmm?"

"Thank you."

"For what?"

"As if you didn't know." She smiled. "Why are you really doing it?"

"As if you didn't know," he said, echoing her words.

"I don't." Maybe she didn't want to know. Or more to the point, didn't want to hope.

"You make it hard to stand on the outside just observing instead of stepping up to help."

That sounded a lot like a compliment and her heart did another flip-floppy thing as she looked at him.

"You're my hero." The words just popped out of her mouth before she could stop them.

It wasn't often he looked surprised, but he did now. "Even though I'm judgmental, pigheaded and sometimes don't know when to stop talking?"

She shrugged. "Heroes are imperfect. Maybe that's why the heroic stuff stands out. They do the right thing in spite of the flaws."

He nodded. "I'm going before you change your mind about that."

This time when he walked away she didn't follow even though she was still confused. He implied that he was helping out for her. What did that mean? Maybe he respected what she was trying to do, but she wasn't sure that he liked her. He definitely didn't trust her. Why would he do anything for her that was so heroically above and beyond the call of duty?

Just when she thought she had him all figured out he had to go and change the rules.

* * *

The next day Cal drove away from Em's place with her beside him in the passenger seat. He glanced sideways and noted that she looked pensive.

"I appreciate you going with me to pick out a gift for Mitch and Sam's baby."

"How could I say no after you played guardian angel last night?"

"What happened to hero?" he asked, glancing over at her.

"That, too." She met his gaze for a second, but his teasing hadn't chased away her tension. "Are you sure your mom's going to be okay with Annie?"

He continued to the entrance of the 95 Freeway and got on, seamlessly merging into northbound traffic. "Absolutely. She insisted, especially when I mentioned shopping for Mitch's new baby boy. Mom's been wanting to spend quality time with Annie and this seemed a perfect opportunity."

"I kind of got that when she wouldn't take no for an answer."

"That, too." He grinned at her.

"You don't find it ironic that we're shopping for a baby gift and dumped our baby on your mother?"

"No. Besides the fact that Annie's taking a nap, what Mom said made sense. It will be faster and easier to pick out just the right thing by ourselves and she's perfectly capable of babysitting." Something was bugging her and he was in too good a mood to spoil it by persuading her to discuss what was on her mind. Better to change the subject. "Isn't it amazing that we're both off today?"

"It's a good thing you are after the night you had."

"Yeah."

It *had* been a long night and not just because of looking in on Henry. Since Lucy and Patty's place was crowded with Jonas there, Cal had commandeered Em's couch to snag some z's whenever he could. It wasn't often considering that the apartment smelled like her. Between looking in on Henry and thinking about Emily's soft, sweet skin and how exciting it would be to touch her everywhere, sleep had been elusive.

Just before dawn Annie had awakened him when she'd grabbed his nose in her chubby little fingers. It was the first time he'd had a chance to watch her toddle happily around first thing in the morning and that energized him somehow. Then his mom had called to see if he still wanted her to help him shop for a baby gift, which had evolved into her watching Annie.

He glanced sideways and noticed that Em looked uncomfortable. At the risk of spoiling his mood, he asked, "What's wrong?"

"So many things, so little time."

"Pick one," he suggested.

"Can I have two?"

"Knock yourself out."

"Actually number one is how your mom will hold up with our little bundle of energy, and I have to bow to your wisdom on that." She twisted her fingers together in her lap.

"What's number two?"

"Are you sure it's okay to leave Henry?"

They'd already been through this and he got the distinct impression that she was creating speed bumps to this shopping expedition where none existed. "Technically we're not leaving Henry. He's being well cared for by his mother and father."

"That's not what I meant." She met his gaze. "Is it okay for you to be away?"

"Yes."

She looked at him expectantly. "Care to elaborate?"

"Kids bounce back incredibly fast. You don't need an M.D. after your name to see that he was feeling his oats this morning. That kid is high-energy and he's got the battle scars to prove it.

Frankly, the hardest thing for Patty and Jonas will be to keep him quiet. They don't need extra people around stirring him up."

"You're sure?"

He glanced over and briefly met her gaze. "First do no harm. Words every doctor lives by. You watch, wait and intervene when necessary. Last night was all about watching and waiting. I was there if he needed anything, which is what would have happened if he'd stayed overnight in the hospital. He was quiet in the E.R. but you never know if that's part of the trauma or just a symptom of a new and scary environment. It's my job to make the call about whether or not skilled observation is indicated. I believe in erring on the side of caution. Patty and Jonas felt they could handle it. Fortunately, they were right and today, except for the sutures in his forehead, you'd never know he took a header yesterday." He briefly met her gaze before looking at the road again. "I wouldn't be here now if it wasn't okay."

"Wow, that was quite a speech." She smiled just a little. "I guess it goes with the new wheels."

"I was wondering when you were going to notice." He'd traded "the princess" in for this Lexus SUV. "There was nowhere for Annie in the other car since it was a two-seater and she couldn't sit in the front. This is more kid-friendly."

"A family vehicle," she said, a tinge of wistfulness in her voice.

That was the second time in two days that she'd mentioned family. It wasn't something he had an answer for and decided saying nothing was the best way to do no harm.

He exited at Lake Mead Boulevard, turned left and crossed over the freeway, then made a left-hand turn into the shopping center where the baby warehouse store was located. It was hard to miss what with the humongous giraffe on the outside of the building.

They parked in front, then entered the store. He looked around at the overwhelming inventory of kid stuff and shook his head.

"I don't know where to start," he admitted.

"I'm shocked and appalled."

"If this were an emergency situation you'd get to feel that way. But I'm completely out of my element. It's why I brought you along. Any suggestions?"

"Do you know if Sam and Mitch registered here?" She sighed at his blank look. "For gifts. Like prospective brides and grooms, expectant moms and dads register their product preferences with a store for shower gifts or even after the baby is born so that anyone wishing to purchase something will know what to get."

"Did you do that with Annie?"

She nodded, but instead of pleasure in the memory, her expression turned pensive. "Sophia threw a baby shower and I registered here."

"Then you know how to check and see if Mitch and Sam did."

"I do."

"Lead the way." He followed her to a computer terminal and they plugged in the names, but couldn't find any information.

"I guess we're flying blind, then," she said. "Let's start in the infant section, zero to six months."

There was an abundance of equipment for keeping infants happy. Papasan infant seat on a frame. Soothing Motions glider. Cradle swing with batteries to keep it moving. He was skeptical of the Jumperoo, a circular frame with a seat in the center.

It was green. "I like the color, but am philosophically opposed to the concept."

"In what way?" she asked.

"Babies need to be free to move around and develop large-muscle skills. If they're confined in something like this for too long a period of time, that can't happen."

Em looked at him. "Annie's pediatrician warned me about that."

"Great minds," he said.

They walked up and down several aisles filled with clothes, bottles, nursing pillows and racks of tiny nail clippers, thermometers and plastic baby bottles. Emily stopped and picked up some sort of sling. There was a tender look on her face.

"I had one of these," she said.

He'd seen new mothers with them and the infant swaddled close to their body. "Did it work for you?"

"Keeps the baby close and hands free," she said softly. "I can't believe she's too big for it now. Seems like yesterday she was tiny enough to tie her to me or put her down and I'd know where she was when I came back. Now she's all over the place and into everything."

"While we're here, maybe we should get some of this stuff so I can safety proof your place and mine."

"Okay."

They passed strollers, cribs, furniture and finally stopped in the toy section. There was a Melodies & Lights Gym floor pad with a tentlike frame containing hanging toys and spinning butterflies that fit over it. Then he spotted two things he had to get.

Cal picked up a red-plastic medical case and read the contents: blue disposable gloves, neon bandages, two-by-two gauze pads, antiseptic wipes and hand gels.

"It's a doctor kit. Mitch will get a kick out of this even if the little guy is too young to appreciate it." He grabbed two more.

"You're buying three?" Em looked puzzled. "Is one for Annie?"

"Yeah," he said. "And I think Henry might like one, too."

"Very sweet of you."

"I'm glad you approve. And before you say anything I'm

planning to get something for Oscar or it wouldn't be fair." He went to a display of T-shirts for new parents and looked them over. One had the Superman design with the word *Dad* inside it. Another said *New Dad*. And he picked up the winner that proclaimed Dad Survived Delivery. "I'm getting this for Mitch. He's been a basket case waiting for Sam to have that baby."

"It's pretty exciting—" She stopped and before she turned away he thought there was a sheen of tears in her eyes.

"Em?" Cal saw her shoulders tense. "What is it? And don't say it's nothing because you've been acting weird since we got in the car."

"It's just—" She turned and rubbed a finger beneath her nose.

"Seriously. I'm not kidding." He'd have pointed a finger at her but his hands were full. "What's bothering you?"

"Looking at all this stuff makes me sad."

He glanced around at the pastel and bright primary colors, the soft cheery wall hangings along with baby blankets and was mystified. "Why? In addition to Disneyland, this has got to be one of the happiest places on earth."

"Not the last time I was here." She sighed and sad eyes looked into his. "I was pregnant and alone. My fault. I get that."

He hadn't brought her along for revenge. He was way over that now. Being a dad to Annie left no energy for anything but moving forward, wherever that took him. "I didn't mean to upset you."

"I know." She shrugged. "I can't help it. You're not the only one who missed out. Bringing Annie into the world was amazing, but it would have been so much richer in memories if you'd shared the experience with me."

"Okay. Here's what we're going to do." He set down the medical kits and T-shirt, then nudged her chin up with his knuckle. "We both made mistakes, but right here, right now we put the past away and start fresh. We start sharing the experience of raising our daughter. You and me—we're going to pick out something for her together."

"I think that's a great idea." Em brushed away a tear from the corner of her eye and smiled.

She looked so beautiful at that moment. His chest got tight and his pulse throbbed. Making peace with her wasn't problem free. Parenting together meant spending time with Em as well as his daughter. Annie was a joy. The magnitude of his wanting for Em was not.

God help him, it was like waiting for the other shoe to fall. Again.

Chapter Eleven

Emily could understand why Cal had asked her to help him shop for a baby gift, but the invitation to tag along when he delivered it was beyond her ability to rationalize. All she could think was that he wanted to show off Annie and didn't trust himself alone with her yet. However, the confidence he displayed while holding newborn Lucas Tenney could make a case for her being wrong, which she very much wanted to be. A very large part of her wanted to believe he'd asked her to come along because he liked spending time with her.

The couple had recently bought a new house in the McDonald Highlands development in Henderson. It was a sprawling two-story with curving staircases and panoramic views of the golf course from the plush green sectional where they were gathered in the family room. Gift paper littered the floor as Samantha Ryan Tenney eagerly and enthusiastically ripped into the gifts Cal had brought.

The brown-eyed blonde held up the toy medical kit. "Look, Mitch. This is too cute."

Her dark-haired husband laughed. "Yeah, nothing like putting pressure on the kid to follow in his father's footsteps."

"It's not a bad life." Cal looked around at the high ceiling, river-rock fireplace and huge kitchen with stainless-steel appliances. "You're doing okay. And with the practice expanding, we stand to be pretty successful."

"Don't get me wrong," Mitch protested. "I love what I do. It's about time the south valley had a facility and they finally will with Mercy Medical Center finishing construction on the third campus."

"It won't be long until the structure is ready, but that's the easy part," Cal said.

"It doesn't look easy," Emily commented. "I've been by the construction on the 215 and Durango and it looks pretty complicated."

"That's all about building codes and passing fire department specifications." Mitch shook his head. "After that it's getting down to the nitty gritty details of policies, procedures and protocols. Budget. Equipment. Before that they need to pass inspections and get certification for radiology, blood gas lab. The personnel needs to be in place. Our own Jake Andrews is a candidate for Trauma Medical Coordinator."

"You didn't tell me that," Sam said, surprised.

Mitch indicated his son. "I've had a few other things on my mind."

"Like birth?" she said, one eyebrow arching. "That must have been hard on you."

"It was. Cal knows," he said, his expression pleading with his partner for backup. "I was checking my beeper constantly, waiting for the call."

"Poor you. That was just as mentally challenging as waiting for your water to break and labor contractions to start."

"A little help, buddy. Change the subject," Mitch pleaded, holding up the toy medical kit.

"I got Annie one, too," Cal said without missing a beat. He was standing with the sleeping newborn, swaying back and forth. "They can be in therapy together."

As if hearing her name was the signal to turn on her fidgeting, their little girl squirmed to get down.

"Reprieve is over," Em said, watching as her toddler sat beside the wrapping paper and grabbed a box. "Don't worry, I'm on full alert so she doesn't turn your lovely home into a postapocalyptic wasteland."

Mitch grinned. "Are you saying that we should enjoy this time before Lucas becomes mobile?"

"That's exactly what I'm saying," she agreed.

"In spite of the fact that he wakes up every two or three hours to eat, and we'd very much like him to grow out of that?" Sam asked.

"I guess that's the definition of conflict," Em said wistfully. "You want them to be normal and grow and learn. Yet this time when you have a chance to protect them passes by in a heartbeat."

She glanced at Cal who was staring at the infant and wondered what was going through his mind. Was he thinking about missing out on seeing Annie at the same age? He wasn't the only one missing out. More and more Em was seeing how Cal embraced being a father. How things might have been if she'd given him an opportunity to screw up before judging him not willing to take responsibility.

"A chance is what it's all about." Mitch watched Annie as she pounded the box lid up and down chattering away.

Then he turned his gaze on his son. "Sometimes a life doesn't even get that."

Sam's expression turned sympathetic and tender. "This is a time to look forward, not back."

"What are you talking about?" Cal asked.

"My first wife decided to discontinue birth control without a discussion when we were having problems. She got pregnant but the trouble didn't go away, so she decided to get rid of the baby, also without discussion. I hate that my child never had a chance."

"Oh, Mitch, I'm so sorry—" Clearly Em wouldn't win a communicator of the year award, but at least she'd tried to tell Cal. And as sad as it made her to not know how her first child was getting along in this world, at least he was in this world with a chance at life.

"How come I didn't know about that?" Cal asked, frowning.

"The marriage ended and there wasn't any reason to bring it up." Mitch shrugged, then smiled tenderly at his wife. "At least not until my tenacious conflict-resolution counselor made me."

"When he says tenacious, he means pit bull," Sam explained. "But we certainly did have our conflicts to resolve. It wasn't easy sailing for us."

"You also have a healthy and handsome little guy," Cal said, smiling down at the little guy in question who was squeaking and squirming in his arms. "Did you know that Em is running a program called Helping Hands that mentors teenage moms who don't get any support from their families?"

"Really?" Sam looked genuinely interested.

Em nodded. "I have two girls right now. The housing was donated by Ginger Davis, president and founder of The Nanny Network. Donations and grant money subsidize what the girls make. They share child care and juggle college classes and part-time jobs. But the program gives them another alternative when an unplanned pregnancy occurs."

She glanced at Cal who was studying her. Instead of resentment or disapproval in his expression, she swore there was pride.

"Em is doing a really good thing for those girls," he commented. "She has specific rules, one of which is getting an education. It's the only way to become an independent member of society and not a drain on taxpayers. The girls work hard. One of them is coparenting with her son's father who is also working hard while he goes to school. Jonas has a good head on his shoulders."

"What an incredible load he's carrying." Sam pulled Annie into her lap when the little girl stood beside her to check out the toys on the sofa.

"That's for sure," Cal agreed. "And it's why the kids need encouragement and assistance. When Henry had an accident, everyone pulled together for him."

"Including Cal," Em told them. "He was there to make sure there were no complications."

"Sounds like an extended family." Sam smiled as Annie squirmed to get down.

"Something I never had," Em said quietly. Everyone looked at her expectantly and she found herself saying more. "It was only my mother and me. My father disappeared before I was born so when things happened there wasn't any support system."

Sam nodded. "I guess we're all broken in some way or other. I lost my mom when I was little and was raised by a stepfather. It wasn't easy, and I hate to spout clichés, but what doesn't kill us makes us stronger. If we're lucky, someone special comes along and we don't have to be quite as strong as we were without them. I waited a very long time for Mitch."

"And wasn't I worth the wait?" he said grinning.

She leaned her head on his shoulder. "Definitely."

Em realized Cal was the only one who hadn't shared part of his past. She knew he'd had a pretty carefree childhood, but he'd also been married and never talked about it. That was part of who he was and she had a bad feeling that it had a lot to do with his never-get-serious-or-take-responsibility attitude.

When she studied him she saw something restless in his eyes, an expression that looked a lot like envy. It occurred to her that she recognized it because of a similar feeling.

Mitch and Sam had revealed that they'd been through a lot before finding each other. Their perseverance had produced a happy marriage and beautiful child. Like Cal, Emily envied them. The family they had was all she'd ever wanted.

If she'd persevered in telling Cal that she was pregnant with his child, maybe they would have had a chance. But whatever broken part of her had kept the secret had cost her that chance. This glimpse of how wonderful their life could have been was her punishment for screwing up.

Several days after her visit to see Mitch and Sam's beautiful baby boy Em was still feeling down, depressed and restless at the same time. It was after 10:00 p.m. and Annie was sound asleep. Em had decided to channel the edgy energy into the distasteful chores that needed doing.

In her cutoff sweatpants and thin-strapped T-shirt she'd already scrubbed the bathrooms and now she had the refrigerator in her crosshairs. With the trash can in front of the open door she was tossing everything that had been there for a week or more.

Peeking underneath the folding top of a square carton that had been chow mein when Cal brought it over she wrinkled her nose at what now looked like a science experiment gone horribly wrong. Next she pulled out a rectangular plastic container with burgers and hot dogs left over after Cal had grilled them. She smiled, remembering how she'd teased him about cooking enough to feed a Third World country.

Something squeezed tight in her chest when she looked at the longneck bottle of beer that he'd stuck in the fridge when Annie had snagged his attention. Apparently she'd needed him more than he'd needed the beer because he never got back to it.

Em picked up the bottle and circled the mouth with the tip of her finger at the same time an image of Cal formed with his big body filling up her tiny kitchen. He was wearing his cocky grin, the one that made her hormones go into free fall and opened a big, lonely, black hole inside her that caused ripples of pain that went clear to her soul. The refrigerator light backlit the bottle as her fingers squeezed until her knuckles turned white. She was the world's biggest idiot.

In every women's magazine on the newsstand there was an article about how to find a good man. She'd actually had the blind luck to stumble across one, then proceeded to throw him back into the pond because she'd been afraid of rejection.

"You're a pathetic loser, Emily Summers." Unable to part with the bottle, she put it back on the shelf and closed the door. "A pathetic, *immature* loser."

She walked down the hall to Annie's room and looked in on her daughter who didn't seem to mind that her mother was an immature loser. At least not yet. Hopefully she'd respect and admire her mother more than Em had her own. Maybe the fact that Cal was involved in his child's life would make Annie's world happier than her own had been even though the perfect family wasn't going to happen.

Em glanced at the watch on her wrist and hoped that ten-thirty was late enough and she was finally tired enough to sleep. In the living room to shut off the lights, she heard a soft knock on the door. The sound made her jump because it was so unexpected this time of night. Probably Lucy or Patty needed to tell her something and didn't want the phone to wake Annie.

She twisted the deadbolt then opened the door, but instead of her neighbors, the owner of that old, flat beer in her refrigerator stood there. Cal. Heart pounding, she said something completely witty and brilliant. "Hi—"

"It's late, I know. But I saw your lights on and—"

Usually he called to tell her he was coming by to see Annie. She studied his face, the deep lines on either side of his nose and mouth that indicated he was tired. Or stressed. Or both. "Is something wrong?"

"I just wanted to look in on Annie. Sorry to bother you, but—"

"It's not a problem." He was in blue scrubs and she guessed that he'd probably come straight here from Mercy Medical Center. That meant he'd worked later than usual. Opening the door wider, she stepped back. "Come in."

"Thanks."

She put her hand on his arm when he started past her. "Annie's asleep, so—"

"I won't wake her. I just want to look at her, to—"

He stopped because his voice cracked. And that wasn't all. Studying him more closely she swore that he looked like a man who was cracking from the inside out. "What's wrong, Cal?" she asked again.

"I'll just be a minute," he said, not answering the question.

She followed him into Annie's room and the night-light revealed the suffering in his eyes as he gently ran his hand over his little girl's curls. Sighing in her sleep, Annie rolled to her tummy with her tush in the air. He ran his finger over her chubby arm and settled his palm on her back, watching it rise and fall. Finally he sighed heavily and moved away from the crib, pausing briefly in the doorway for a last look before walking into the living room.

He stopped by the coffee table and shoved his fingers

through his hair. "Thanks, Em. I appreciate you not giving me a hard time."

"Don't thank me just yet." In her opinion she'd never given him a hard time about seeing Annie. A guilty conscience tends to make you gracious and agreeable even if you were opposed to a father/daughter relationship, which she was not. But he'd never stopped by this late or looked this troubled. "I want to know what happened to you."

He turned to look at her. "What makes you think anything happened?"

"And here I thought that being a doctor made you brighter than the average guy—"

His laugh was bitter. "Not so much."

When he moved toward the door to leave, she rushed around him and stood in front of it. "Not so fast."

For the first time the smallest hint of a smile showed at the corners of his mouth. "What are you doing?"

"I'm not letting you leave until you talk to me."

"What if I don't want to talk?"

"I have my ways." She folded her arms beneath her breasts and saw the movement draw his gaze there followed by a deep swallow. "Now, tell me why it was so important that you see Annie."

He took her measure and finally nodded. "I needed to make sure she was all right. That she's healthy, breathing, happy and normal."

Oh, no. "You lost a patient, didn't you?"

He nodded miserably. "A little girl. Three years old. Car accident. Depressed skull fracture and abdominal injuries."

"Oh, Cal—I'm so sorry."

"We stabilized her in the E.R. and she made it into surgery but Jake lost her on the table." Misery clouded his eyes. "The thing is the parents did everything right. She was in the car seat, properly secured in the back passenger seat. Their SUV was broadsided by a pickup that didn't stop for a red light."

"It's not your fault," Em said firmly.

"No?" He shook his head. "I didn't do enough. I must have missed something or I wouldn't have lost her."

"You're not God."

"Don't you think I know that?" He curved his fingers around her upper arms. "If I were all powerful, I'd be able to protect kids. I could stop the things people do to each other. The lies, manipulation. They break the rules of human decency. If I were God, I'd be able to save innocent lives from the bad stuff."

He was talking in generalities, but there was something in his eyes, in his voice, in his expression that told her whatever he was feeling was profoundly personal. And not necessarily about the little girl he'd lost, but something innocent in himself that had died.

"You're a good man and a good doctor." The words didn't take away the pain and grief in his expression.

"I hate to lose," he ground out.

"But you can't always win."

Em was desperate to reassure him and didn't know what to do except press her body to his and put her arms around him offering him comfort through her touch. She felt the tension in his body and tightened her grip, resting her head on his chest, feeling the powerful pounding of his heart beneath her cheek.

She felt the conflict rage in him and his resistance to her reassurance but held on until he pressed his hand to the back of her head and his fingers tangled in her hair. Gently he tugged, tilting her face up.

"Em—"

The agonized whisper of her name on his lips was the last

thing he said before lowering his mouth to hers. The touch unleashed all the storm of need inside her and drowned rational thought, silencing all the reasons why this was not a good idea. Greedily his mouth took hers, sending jolts of excitement arcing through her that fried her nerve endings.

He traced her bottom lip with his tongue and she opened. Without hesitation he dipped inside and eagerly took what she offered. He kissed her cheek, her jaw, the sensitive place just beneath her ear and down her neck.

Breathing hard, he swung her into his arms and said in a voice that scraped over her skin and made her tingle, "I want you, Em. If you have a problem with that, speak now—"

She touched her fingertip to his mouth and shook her head. "You'll get no argument from me."

Looking fierce and so very wonderful, he said, "That would be a first."

"Not true." She locked her arms around his neck as he carried her into her room. "I'm not a confrontational sort of woman."

"Yes, you are." He stopped by her bed and removed his arm from behind her legs, letting them slide down his front until her bare toes brushed the carpet. "But I don't need sparks of conflict to build a fire." His heated gaze seared to her soul as he stared down. "All I need is to look at you."

He took the bottom of her T-shirt and slowly slid it up and over her raised arms and satisfaction glittered in his eyes. "Pay dirt. You're not wearing a bra."

"I didn't think I had to," she said.

"Not on my account."

His gaze darkened when he touched the red discoloration on her breast, all that remained of the lump. Bending slightly, he tenderly kissed it and she nearly dissolved from the liquid heat that surged through her. While his lips had their way with her breasts, his thumbs hooked in the elastic waistband of her shorts and pushed down. When they pooled at her feet, she stepped out of them and stood before him completely naked except for the watch on her wrist.

He slid his palm over her abdomen, then dipped a finger into the curls between her legs, his breath catching as he felt her waiting warmth. Her thighs quivered and practically begged for more. With one sweeping movement, he pushed her comforter down until the sheets beneath beckoned them. Then he yanked off his scrubs, retrieving his wallet from the back pocket and setting it on her nightstand.

Em crawled onto the bed and waited for him to join her, watching him lift a condom from his wallet. He opened the foil packet and covered himself. Need and intensity glittered in his eyes as he put one knee on the mattress and braced his hands on either side of her, trapping her in the most sensuous and sexy possible way.

Breathing hard, he settled on top of her and she gloried in being beneath him. He pushed inside and filled her. It was like she was finally where she belonged with who she was meant to be with.

He buried his face in her neck and slowly moved in and out, each thrust sending her higher, stoking the tension building within her. Every stroke intensified the pressure until finally she shattered and pleasure punched through her very center, rippling outward to every part of her.

Moments later he went stone still and groaned out his own release, holding her to him as if he'd never let her go. She slid her arms around him and held on tight because she was exactly where she wanted to be.

Where she wanted to stay.

Chapter Twelve

Cal felt Emily shiver from being naked under the air-conditioning vent and pulled the sheet up over them as he snuggled her more securely to his side.

"You know what they say about combining body heat," he said, then brushed his mouth over her forehead.

She rested her arm over his belly, her breasts pressed against him and her only reply was, "Mmm—"

The single sound, not even a word really, was just about the sexiest thing he'd ever heard and parts of him responded. He wanted her again, as much or more than he had when he'd walked in here tonight. He'd needed to see Annie, but deep down inside it was Em he wanted. Some instinct told him that only she could take away, for just a little while, the guilt and pain of losing a kid.

He knew it was way past time to go and there were nine different ways that what he'd just done with Em was wrong.

Right now, with her in his arms and her soft, sweet, satisfie
curves pressed sleepily to his side, he couldn't think abou
that. There would be plenty of opportunity to kick himself si
ways to Sunday, but for now that could wait.

Em put a soft kiss on his shoulder. "How do you feel?"

He turned his head to look at her. The nightstand light wa
behind him but illuminated her face and the sympatheti
concern in her dark eyes. She wasn't asking if the sex wa
good, and he didn't really want to talk about anything else.

He forced a smile. "It's pretty hard to feel bad after that.

"I meant are you still thinking about what happened in th
E.R.?"

He shrugged. "You never get used to it when a young lif
is cut short."

She was quiet for a few moments, but he could almost fee
the energy of her whirling thoughts pumping through her. ∕
frown hinted that the thoughts were troubling.

"Cal, I—"

"Are you going to get serious on me?"

"It's okay for you, but I'm supposed to be the good-tim
girl?" she said.

"I didn't mean it like that."

"Sure you did." She brushed a finger over his abdomen an
his muscles tensed involuntarily. "But I demand equal time.

"Okay. Go."

"I've been thinking about what you said before we—yo
know."

It surprised him that she was still shy. She had always bee
that way afterward, but when their bodies were giving an
taking her passion and responsiveness always blew him away
"We had sex."

"Yeah. That." She wouldn't meet his gaze.

"I said a lot of things. What specifically?"

"About hating to lose."

He nodded. "It's true. Obviously losing a patient is unacceptable to any doctor and that's especially the case with children. But I'm competitive in most ways. When I played sports it was running up the score. In school it was about having the highest grade point average. Being a doctor means saving my patients."

"What about being married?" she asked out of the blue.

"What do you mean?"

"How do you judge success in marriage?" She met his gaze. "Your father told me you were married once. When I had questions, he said I'd have to ask you. So, I'm asking."

When he sat up the sheet pulled away, revealing her breasts, the softly feminine flesh he'd just touched and kissed, the healing scar from her recent procedure. Looking around he noticed the softly feminine pink-and-lavender floral print comforter and lace crisscross curtains over the blinds on the windows. Even the dangly crystals sparkling on the lampshades marked this room as a girly space.

A space that he should never have set foot in, but regret and remorse didn't stop him from wanting her again. It stirred within him, even now when she was asking about failures he spent every day trying to forget.

He threw the sheet back and stood then found his scrubs and dressed. When she joined him in the living room she'd put on a short yellow terrycloth robe that hid her nakedness but didn't erase the memories of her body that were branded into his mind.

She walked past him and stood in front of the door as she'd done just a little while ago. "Obviously I touched a nerve."

"It's not a time I enjoy talking about."

"Maybe if you did it wouldn't have as much power over you."

Staring at her, he put his hands on his hips. "So your diagnosis and treatment are to use my words?"

"I'm not minimizing your experience, but you might feel better."

Maybe she was right. Not about feeling better, but about talking. It was time to tell her, let her know that he wasn't just a judgmental jerk and had good reason for his feelings.

He blew out a long breath. "It happened when I was just nineteen."

"So young—"

When she caught her top lip between her teeth, he fixed his gaze on the door behind her, the deadbolt. That seemed appropriate. "I was quarterback of the football team and the guy with the highest grade point average in the class. She was homecoming queen and captain of the cheerleading squad. The golden couple."

"What happened?"

"We dated all of senior year. I always knew I wanted to be a doctor. My dad is, and it runs in the family. Lori knew that but when graduation got closer, she started talking about going to the same college, about staying together."

"I understand that."

"She didn't get into the college where I was going. Her grades weren't good enough."

Em shifted her bare feet. "So you married her to be together."

"Not exactly." He stared so hard at the deadbolt the edges got fuzzy. "Just before graduation she told me she was pregnant."

"I see." Her frown said she was lying.

"Being a doctor isn't the only Westen characteristic hard-wired into my DNA. Doing the right thing is right there at the top. Every time I went against that I got burned—from playing with fireworks to BB guns. By the time I'd gone through high school, I'd learned my lesson. Doing the right thing meant marrying the girl carrying my baby, so I did."

"And the baby?" she whispered.

He looked at her then as his stomach knotted. Bitter memories flashed through him and resurrected his rage. "There was no baby."

"What happened to it?"

"There never was a baby," he said, putting a finer point on it. He knew she got the message when her eyes grew wide.

"She lied to you about being pregnant?"

"Pretty much."

"So you divorced her," Em said.

"If only." He ran his fingers through his hair. "See, that's where my moral compass bit me in the ass. In my family when you get married, the right thing is to stay married. So I did."

"But you're not now."

He shook his head. "We stayed together while I went to school, worked and studied. That didn't leave a whole lot of time left over to build a relationship."

"She was unhappy?"

He laughed, but it was a harsh sound, devoid of amusement. "That's a safe bet, although she never once came to me and said she was lonely, neglected and unhappy. I found out when the E.R. called and said my wife had taken pills and tried to kill herself."

Em gasped and touched her fingers to her mouth. "Oh, Cal—but she pulled through?"

"Yeah. That time and every other time she cried out for attention and ended up in the E.R."

"So you finally left her?"

"Nope." If only he thought bitterly. "I was still determined to do the right thing. When I was doing my residency here in Las Vegas at the county hospital, she decided she'd had enough and walked out. No drama. No warning. She just said it was over."

Emily looked confused. "After the lies and the drama, I should think you'd have been relieved."

"You'd think." He grabbed his car keys from the coffee table.

"I'm very sorry that happened to you, Cal."

"What you really mean is that for a smart guy with a GPA somewhere in the stratosphere I was pretty damn dumb."

"No, you were pretty darn noble." She shook her head. "But I can certainly understand why you felt the way you did about—"

"Finding out I had a daughter?"

"Yes," she said, looking pretty guilty.

"I didn't think it was possible to be that stupid again, but I was wrong. The first time, I'd started to love a baby that didn't exist." He moved in front of her and stared down until she stepped aside. "The second time I didn't know a baby existed that I needed to love."

She sucked in a breath. "I'm sorry, Cal."

"You told me you weren't going to say that again."

"I was wrong. It's not the first time and probably won't be the last."

"That makes two of us. I wasted too many years living a lie and promised myself it would never happen again. The truth, the whole truth. Nothing but the truth for me." He opened the door, then glanced over his shoulder at the moisture in her troubled dark eyes.

He closed the door behind him and wondered why he felt like the world's worst bastard. It was time she knew what had happened to him. Maybe he should have told her when they were dating, but he hadn't. Part of him was glad he'd waited until now because it put distance between them. It was a way for her to understand that he'd drawn a line in the sand and why he didn't intend to cross it.

Now there were no secrets.

Except what he felt for Em.

He couldn't stop wanting her and wasn't sure why. The

only thing he was sure of was that there was no win in a relationship with a woman who'd deceived him. If you couldn't win, what was the point of playing? Or maybe that was an excuse because he wasn't willing to take a chance.

Em parked on the top floor of Green Valley Ranch Hotel and Casino's self-parking structure because she knew it wouldn't take an elevator ride to get her where she needed to be. She was late meeting Sophia for dinner at the Grand Café and hurried through the maze of slot-machine lights and sounds, turned right at the Player Rewards Club counter, raced past the water wall at the Feast Buffet and stopped at the restaurant desk to check in with the hostess. The woman in the long-sleeved crisp, white blouse and black pants directed her to a table in the far back corner where the casino noises wouldn't intrude.

She sat down in the booth across from her friend. "Hi. Sorry I'm late."

"No problem." Soph smiled, then sipped red wine.

Em saw the glass of soda water with lime waiting and smiled at the friend who knew her so well. "Thanks."

"You're welcome."

The waitress came and took their salad orders, Cobb for Em and chicken Caesar for Sophia, then left them alone.

"How are things at work?" Em asked.

"I love my job. The children are adorable and so normal." Her gray eyes clouded over for a moment, but a new and recent concern pushed away the memories. "But I need to ask you something."

"Shoot."

"What's going on with Patty?"

"The usual. She has a toddler while working and going to school and juggling a relationship with her child's father." Em realized that two out of those three applied to her. The only difference was she didn't have to contend with school. "Why?"

"Are she and Jonas having problems?"

"Not that I'm aware of. But I haven't had a real heart-to-heart talk with her for a while. We've both been busy." If anyone should win man-problems-of-the-year award, it was Em. Considering she'd slept with her child's father. Again. And he all but gave her the brush off. None of which she wanted to think about, let alone discuss. It just hurt too much. But concentrating on someone else would take her mind off her own imploding life. "What makes you think Patty and Jonas are going through something, Soph?"

"When she was working her shift I overheard her on the phone. She said his name, so I know he was getting an earful. And the tense tone said it was not in a good way." Sophia frowned. "Not only that, she's been distracted lately. And edgy."

"Is the mood impacting her work?"

"No. She's wonderful with the children." Sophia sipped her wine. "I'm just concerned about her. She's normally so perky that I noticed the difference."

"I can talk to her if you want."

"No. Just keep an eye on her."

"I'll do it," Em promised.

The server brought their salads and after determining there was nothing else they needed and encouraging them to have a nice dinner, she left.

Em picked up her fork and messed up the tidy rows of bacon, egg, avocado and blue cheese bits. She continued to move the lettuce around without putting any in her mouth. Before Cal had arrived, she'd been pretty hungry. One look at him in his jeans and T-shirt had pretty much destroyed her appetite.

It was the first she'd seen him since the night he'd taken her to bed and loved her until she'd thought she would drown in the pleasure. The first time since he'd pulled the rug out from under her with revelations of his past. A little while ago he'd come over after calling, then volunteering to stay with Annie while Em had a relaxing night out. Awkwardness and tension had rolled off him in waves and now relaxing just wasn't going to happen.

"I feel weird without Annie."

Sophia stared across the table. "Yeah. What's up with that? We picked this place because it's nice but casual and kid-friendly. For Annie. How come I'm not seeing my goddaughter right now?"

"Let me add another sorry to the one you got because I was late. Cal wanted to spend time with her and it seemed like a good idea."

"Because you feel guilty?" Sophia asked.

"Because he's a fantastic father."

"And how are things between you and Doctor Do Good?"

"Oh, you know—"

Sophia gave her a wry look before awareness sparked in her eyes. "That's eerily similar to what you said the last time you didn't want to tell me what was going on with you and Cal. And for the record, it doesn't ease my mind."

Em remembered that afternoon in Sophia's office when she didn't want to tell her friend that she'd slept with Cal. Suddenly she felt as if she were stuck in a bad sci-fi movie where she couldn't get out of a dangerous time loop and kept repeating destructive behavior.

"Cal and I are coparenting Annie. That's all there is to that."

"You slept with him again, didn't you?" Sophia's gray eyes narrowed.

Sophia was her best friend, but that was good news and

bad. The club soda and lime waiting for her tonight was good, but this way she had of reading minds was not.

Unfortunately lying through her teeth to her BFF wasn't good, either.

"Yes, we slept together, but it's not what you think."

"Putting aside what I think for now, let me just ask this. Have you even heard the phrase *just say no?*"

"It's not that simple."

"You're wrong. Single syllable. Practice it. *N-O*. Easy."

"For you maybe. But nothing about Cal Westen has ever been easy for me."

"What happened?" Sophia chewed a bite of salad.

"He stopped by without calling, which is very unlike him. Said he just wanted to see Annie. He wouldn't wake her, and he didn't. He just put his hand on her back, to make sure she was okay." Em sipped her club soda. "He was really upset after losing a kid in the E.R. Someone ran a stop sign and hit the SUV. He really took it hard."

"I can understand that." Sophia's expression turned dark.

"I had to do something for him," Em said.

"So you slept with him?"

"You make it sound calculated. I just put my arms around him. It was all I could think of to comfort him." Em shrugged. "After that I'm not exactly sure how we ended up in bed. It sort of just happened. Please don't lecture me. I know it wasn't smart, but I couldn't seem to stop myself."

"Yeah, I understand how that feels, too." Her friend pushed the lettuce around her plate. "It's all fun and games until someone gets hurt."

"Soph, I found out about his baggage."

"What?"

Em told her about the pregnancy lie, the marriage and suicide attempts before his wife simply walked out.

"It sounds like a nightmare," Sophia said.

"Yeah. It helps me to understand why he said what he did when I tried to tell him I was pregnant."

"His past makes it okay for him to be a jerk?" Sophia picked up her fork again and speared a crouton.

"You're being pretty heartless," Em accused.

"I'm realistic. I can do that because I'm not emotionally involved with an emotionally unavailable man."

"What are you talking about?"

"Remember I told you that if he wanted you to know about his past he'd tell you?"

"I asked," Em said. She hadn't thought it was possible for her stomach to twist into more knots, but it did when she saw the expression on her friend's face. "What?"

"Think about it, Em. Why now? You went out with him for six months before you got pregnant. At any time during that period did he share personal information?"

"No. After establishing that we were both single, he'd either dodge questions about his past or change the subject."

"Why didn't he dodge the question or change the subject this time? After sex, I might add."

After sex the second time to be more precise, Em thought. As if the first time was a fluke, but time number two made it a pattern he didn't want. The impact of what her friend was saying hit her hard.

"He's *deliberately* pushing me away," Em whispered.

"That would be my guess," Sophia agreed.

Em could hardly breathe as the realization sat like a boulder on her chest. All this time since coming clean about having Cal's baby, she'd been blaming herself for the fact that he would never trust and love her only to find out that a woman had destroyed his trust when he was most vulnerable, not to mention impressionable. That was before Em had ever met him. The truth was she'd never had a chance to win his heart, even before she'd messed up.

Sophia studied her intently. "Please don't tell me you've fallen in love with him."

"No."

"Good."

Em sat back in the booth and dropped her hands into her lap. "Technically I never *stopped* loving him."

"Oh, Em—"

"And we share a child that we're both committed to coparenting. This time it won't be so easy to put him out of my mind." Not that Em had ever successfully done that. "I'll have to see him all the time. I'm going to have to watch the parade of women in his life, and so will Annie. I wanted so much better for her than I had."

"At least she'll know her father and not have to wonder about him," Sophia offered.

"Maybe." Em smiled weakly. "No one knows better than me that life isn't perfect. But I vowed that my children would have two parents who were together. A couple. What happened to my dream?"

"You fell in love," Sophia said.

Instead of finding happily ever after she found heartbreak. Maybe ignorance *was* bliss. Maybe she would have been better off not knowing about his past because the truth meant he'd never let himself care again.

In this case honesty was not the best policy.

Chapter Thirteen

After putting Annie to sleep Cal sat on Em's light green sofa with his feet propped on her cherrywood coffee table and used her remote to flip through the TV channels. At least she had more than when he'd first met her.

Emily Summers hated electronics of any kind and barely tolerated computers. When they'd been together before, he'd hooked up her DVD player and HD cable box so they'd have more visual choices, not that they'd spent much time doing that. His body tightened painfully as memories of their intimate alternative entertainment activities flashed through his mind. After that a flash of something else zapped him when he wondered who'd hooked everything up for her after moving to this apartment.

It was none of his business; that was the past and didn't matter. As soon as the message got from his gut to his head everything would be fine. Great. Fan-freaking-tastic.

He'd lost count of how many times he'd checked the Sci-fi channel and ESPN hoping he'd missed something good even though he'd come up empty.

That could be a metaphor for his life. *Empty* summed it up pretty well. Except for Annie he only had a revolving door of relationships that were meaningless exercises in companionship and simply filled his free time. He only felt alive, stimulated and content with Em and that was damned annoying.

He flipped the TV off and tossed the remote on the couch beside him, then leaned down and picked up the five throw pillows in shades of green, beige and maroon that his daughter had delighted in throwing on the floor. He smiled, remembering the way she'd giggled and made a game out of it. When he picked them up, she threw them down again.

He'd made a lot of progress with his daughter in the last two months. She knew him and there'd only been a couple of rough spots tonight. The first had been when Annie watched her mother leave. The bitterly unhappy crying still had the power to rip his heart out, but he knew how she felt because Em had once left him. He'd been bitter and unhappy about it.

After checking on his little girl who was sleeping like a baby, he wandered into the kitchen and absently opened the refrigerator. On the top shelf was a beer—an opened, half-empty beer. He must have stuck it in there because Em didn't drink. But why hadn't she thrown it out?

Glancing around the apartment he realized this felt more like home than his huge house on the golf course. Pale gold gave the place a charming warmth. The yellow pottery bowl filled with apples, bananas and oranges added a touch of color on the bar. Photos, mostly of Annie, were scattered around on every flat surface and there were some hanging on the walls. Lately this small two-bedroom, two-bath apartment was the only place he wanted to be. With Em.

He glanced at his watch and noted that it was eight twenty-five, a full seven minutes later than the last time he'd checked. Was she out with a guy? She'd only said she was going to meet a friend for dinner and was taking Annie until he'd offered to watch his daughter. Had he handed her the opportunity for a more intimate date with another guy?

"No." He said it out loud and with a force that was surprising. "Can't be *another* guy because that would imply she already had one. Which would be me and that's not what's going on."

He heard footsteps outside on the walkway and hurried into the living room to flip the TV back on and settle himself on the sofa with an appropriately relaxed air. And if he could pull that off, he'd get an Academy Award for outstanding performance by a jealous guy who had no right to be.

The deadbolt turned just before the door swung wide and Em was there. "Hi."

"Hey." He stretched and yawned, wondering if that was performance overkill. "Did you have a good time?" In his mind he added, with…? Hoping she'd fill in the blank.

"Yeah." She set her purse on the bar beside the yellow bowl. "How's Annie?"

"Good. We had a great time. Couldn't have been better."

"Did she cry very long after I left?"

He stood and slid his fingertips into the pockets of his jeans as he wandered closer to her. "She was successfully distracted by five-pillow pickup."

"Oh?"

"She threw them on the floor, and I picked them up."

"I know that game. It's one of her favorites." Em met his gaze. "Did she wear you out?"

"Nah." Maybe the yawn *was* too much. "So… Where did you go?" And who did you go with?

"Just dinner. The Grand Café at Green Valley Ranch."

He wanted to shake her into giving him the information. Or kiss her and make her forget anyone but him. More than once she'd teased him about being dumb for a smart guy. This was another one of those times. Kissing her was a very stupid idea. The last kiss had landed them in her bed where he found out for a fact that she still had the same floral comforter he'd once swept onto the floor because he couldn't wait a second longer to have her.

Cal backed away when the sweet scent of her skin tempted him to ignore his common sense. He figured flat-out asking who she'd been with was the only way to find out what he wanted to know.

"So who did you go to dinner with?" he inquired, as casually as possible.

She met his gaze and whatever she saw made her take several steps back. "I met Sophia."

The friend who'd been with Em when Annie was born, he thought. Instantly the tension inside him eased. "How is she?"

"Fine."

He waited for more, but got nothing. "Was it a special occasion?"

"Just catching up." Em shrugged and glanced at the clock. "Look, Cal, I appreciate you watching Annie for me…."

But it's time to go is what she meant. The devil of it was that he wasn't ready to leave. "I figured you'd be out later and there's this movie on HBO."

"It's getting kind of late."

Emily-speak for hit the road. He tried in vain to tamp down his annoyance by telling himself he couldn't have it both ways. Right here in this room he'd pushed her away with the story of his past and shouldn't be so angry that it worked.

"Okay." He grabbed his car keys from the bar. "You're right. I should get going."

Back to the big empty house on the golf course. The mansion that was as boring as the TV season during summer reruns.

Emily followed and they stood in front of the closed door. "Thanks for staying with Annie. It was an unexpected treat to go without a diaper bag. Although I missed her terribly."

And what about me? he wanted to ask. Did you miss me, too?

He looked down at her, the big dark eyes and a mouth that was made for kissing. He curled his fingers into his palms before he reached out for her, to draw her against him. She was behaving exactly as he'd wanted her to and it would be stupid to undo the steps he'd taken.

"Okay, then," he said. "I'll—"

A knock sounded, startling both of them. Em looked puzzled before opening the door. Patty stood there, blue eyes wide with surprise when she saw him.

"Hi—" She looked from him to Em. "I'm sorry. I didn't know you were— I'll come back another time."

"It's okay, Patty." Em glanced up at him. "Cal was just leaving."

"Yeah. I have to go." Because it would be nine kinds of stupid to stay. "Nice to see you, Patty. I'll just—"

A baby cry came from Annie's room. Em looked at the teen. "I need to get her. Can you—"

"I'll go," Cal said. "You guys can talk."

"Are you sure?"

"Completely," he said. "Pretend I'm not here."

He walked into the bedroom and looked in on his daughter. Her eyes were closed and she was on her tummy. She moaned, but he didn't want to pick her up unless absolutely necessary and full-on wake her up. He put his palm on her back and rubbed, gently, soothingly, just to let her know someone was there. Voices drifted to him from the other room and he could hear every word.

"I have to tell you something, and you're not going to like it—" Patty's voice broke on a sob "—I'm pregnant."

"Oh, Patty, no."

"I missed my period and hoped it was just a false alarm. But the pregnancy test was positive. Please don't be mad—"

"I'm not mad."

"It's against the rules," the teen said. "I know that. But we're a family and it was so hard, you know?"

"Yeah. I understand."

"I don't know what I'll do if I have to leave Helping Hands. You always say we have to learn from our mistakes. We didn't mean for this to happen. We were so careful."

Cal understood that. He and Em were poster children for careful and he stared down at the result of being cautious. Birth control wasn't 100 percent foolproof. He was the fool who could swear to that. But when he felt the rise and fall of his daughter's back and watched her so sweet in sleep and remembered her laughter, he didn't feel like a fool. A feeling big and pure welled up inside him that he recognized as love.

"Patty, does Jonas know you're going to have a baby?" Em's voice was firm and calm, not betraying her feelings.

"I can't tell him."

"You have to," Em urged.

"You're going to throw me out," Patty sobbed. "I knew it. And if I tell Jonas he'll leave like Lucy's boyfriend did."

"Jonas loves you." Em's voice softened. "I know it will be hard, but he has a right to know the truth. Being honest is always best."

"Not this time," Patty protested.

"You're wrong. I made a mistake not telling Cal about his daughter. I wish I could take it back, but that's not possible."

"Jonas won't understand."

"He might be angry at first," Em said, "but he'll get over it. He loves Henry. You know that. And he loves you. He'll love this baby, too."

"You always said that one baby is a lot of work. Two is four times as much. How can we work *that* out? We can barely do it now."

"You've got a support system," Em told her. "Me. Jonas. Lucy. Cal—"

Was he part of their little family? He hadn't wanted Em to stay here, but she wouldn't hear of leaving. So, in getting to know his daughter, he'd gotten sucked into this ragtag group.

When he determined Annie was sleeping soundly again, he went into the living room. "I could pretend I didn't hear, but it would be a lie. Em's right about telling the truth."

Both women looked at him before Patty shook her head. "I have to go."

"Wait—" Before Em could stop her she was gone. When she looked up at him her eyes were troubled. "This is a fine mess."

No kidding, he thought.

And he didn't just mean what he'd overheard.

Emily smiled at the gray-haired older man who'd followed her into the hall outside the E.R. trauma bay where his terminally ill wife was now breathing more easily.

She put her hand on his arm. "Mr. Mendenhall, I promise I'll find a place for Esther in hospice care. They'll keep her comfortable."

"That's what I want." His dark eyes turned into black, bottomless pools of sadness. "Esther has taken care of me for over fifty years and now it's my turn to make sure she has what she needs. We've had quantity togetherness and now it's about quality."

"I understand. Mercy Medical Center has a wonderful

skilled nursing facility." She closed the chart. "I'll make some phone calls and make sure there's a bed. Don't worry."

He smiled regretfully. "From your mouth to God's ear."

She turned away and walked down the hall past gurneys, medical machines and laundry carts toward the waiting area and the elevators beyond. Her heart was heavy for so many reasons, not the least of which was trying not to cry for a man and woman who'd spent more than half a century with each other and would soon have to say goodbye.

At least they had those years together. She'd never get a chance to find out what a life with Cal would have been like. And Patty was pregnant which was going to complicate the hell out of the life the teens were working so hard to build. Her vision blurred as moisture filled her eyes and she quickly moved past the information desk and a tall man standing there.

"Emily?"

Oh, for Pete's sake. Why couldn't she have the tiniest little meltdown in private?

She blinked the moisture from her eyes as best she could, brushed the rogue tears from her cheeks, sniffled and turned to see Cal's father. "Ken," she said with as much perkiness as she could. "Nice to see you."

He frowned. "What's wrong?"

"Oh, you know—" She shrugged.

"Is it Annie?"

"No," she cried. "I dropped her off at Cal's—"

"I assume he's there?" his father asked wryly.

She smiled. "He is. I was called in to work and he isn't in the E.R. today. We always try to make sure she's with one of us if possible."

"That's wise," he agreed.

"That's us. The cool parents—"

When her voice caught, he took her elbow and guided her around the corner from the E.R. into a quiet hallway. "No one's around. You can tell me what you're upset about."

"How much time have you got?" she asked, trying to joke her way out of talking.

"As much as you need. I'm here to see a patient, then I have the afternoon off." He leaned a broad shoulder against the wall. "Spill it, young lady. Is it work? You came from the E.R."

The man wasn't giving her a choice. "I just came from talking with the spouse of a patient facing a terminal illness."

"I'm sorry. That's never easy." He looked sympathetic even as he asked, "What else is bothering you?"

"One of the teens in my program just found out she's having another baby, a second unplanned pregnancy."

"I see."

"The thing is, I tried so hard to get the message across to the girls that we all make mistakes, but we can learn from them." She looked up at him. "I'm the wrong person to be telling them what to do."

"Why would you say that?" he asked.

"I'm a failure. I always have been. I have no business trying to be a role model to these girls. It makes me a do-as-I-say-not-as-I-do kind of person. They at least had the guts to keep their babies. I gave mine away—"

"That's not true. You're raising Annie. Very well, in my opinion."

She pressed the chart in her hand against her chest. "I'm not talking about Annie. When I was fifteen I got pregnant and had a baby boy. My mother gave me a choice—give the baby up for adoption or leave. I tried leaving but the streets are no place to raise a baby and I figured he'd be better off with two parents, somewhere to live and food. Call me crazy."

"Hardly." His expression was sympathetic. "Do you regret giving your baby up?"

She thought about how to answer. "No. I regret not being in a position to give him the life he deserved. So I stepped aside and let the parents he deserved give him that life. He'd be twelve now, on the verge of being a man and I regret not being able to see him and know that everything is okay." She regretted that the confession made Cal think less of her than he already had, but that wasn't something she'd share with his father. Despite the thought, she met the man's gaze directly. "Under the same circumstances I would do the same thing again."

"But you don't want that to happen to the teens you're mentoring."

It wasn't a question and she appreciated that. "I want them to have more than one choice about what to do if an unplanned pregnancy happens."

Ken nodded. "Then I'm sure you'll help Patty through this difficult time."

"Maybe I'm not the right person to counsel her. After all, I did the same thing."

"Not exactly." He folded his arms over his chest. "The pregnancy with Annie might have been unplanned, but you were in a position to care for her."

Wow. He was defending her to herself. This man should have nothing but resentment and yet he didn't. Like father, like son? Not so much.

"Cal told me about his past."

He frowned and a muscle in his jaw jerked. "I remember when he came to Carol and me with the news that Lori was pregnant. We both advised him to move forward with his plans for school and we'd help Lori with the pregnancy, etcetera. But Cal insisted on getting married. What a disaster."

"He's an incredibly good and decent and special man."

Ken studied her. "I don't think I ever realized before that when you talk about him your face lights up."

"Oh?" Apparently she was going to have to work harder on hiding her feelings.

"I'm Cal's father and certainly his most enthusiastic supporter. But he doesn't walk on water, Emily. In fact, after things didn't work out between the two of you, he was quite the— How should I put this?" He thought for a moment. "Difficult to live with is the most delicate way to phrase it. He takes such pride in being the one to walk away."

"The winner," she said softly. "He hates to lose."

"Exactly."

So she'd hurt his pride, Em thought. That and two dollars would buy her a cup of coffee in the land of lost opportunities. Em knew he'd cared for her once, but she burned that bridge. There was no going back.

"I'm sorry to dump on you," she said. "It's just that the girls I'm trying to help are my family. A shrink would have a field day with me, trying to make a difference because of the one child I desperately wanted and couldn't keep."

"Don't be so hard on yourself, Emily. Everyone makes mistakes. Character is defined by how we deal with the messes we make." He frowned. "I'm quite sure that was something Cal heard growing up and possibly factored into his decision to marry that deceitful witch."

"Don't be so hard on yourself, Ken," she echoed. "How could you know anyone would be so manipulative?"

"Certainly Carol and I had no clue. And Cal stayed with her way past the time when he should have left. It left a mark on him." He shook his head. "Unfortunately that's making him unwilling to take another chance. As you said, he hates to lose. That makes him a good doctor, but I'm afraid his personal life will suffer because of it."

"Yeah—"

He glanced down when the pager on his belt vibrated. After looking at the display, he said, "I have to go."

"Of course. I didn't mean to keep you."

"Not at all." He gave her a quick hug. "Hang in there."

What other choice did she have? she thought, watching him hurry away. He'd raised Cal to be the good man he was, the man she fell in love with, created a child with and fell in love with all over again as she watched him do the right thing by his daughter.

The future stretched in front of her holding nothing but pain because of interacting with him to share Annie. She'd made a mess of her life and standing on the outside looking in was her punishment. She couldn't even say she didn't deserve it.

Chapter Fourteen

Cal sat on the short end of the leather corner group in his family room with Annie in his arms while she drank from her sippy cup. His father had dropped by for a chat and was watching from the other end of the sofa as his relaxed grand-daughter looked around with sleepy blue eyes and absently grabbed a bare foot.

There were times when love for his little girl hit Cal like a tsunami, overwhelming him with its power. This was one of those times and it seemed fitting that his dad was here.

"It's not like you to stop by without calling, Dad. I'm glad I was here."

"It wasn't a whim. I ran into Emily at Mercy Medical Center. She said you were watching Annie. For the record it's not you I'm here to visit."

"Wow. I feel cherished." Cal grinned when his father rolled his eyes. "How's mom?"

"Fine. Shopping for our trip to Alaska."

"When are you guys going?"

"A few weeks." He shrugged. "Your mother could probably tell you when down to the hour and second."

"She's looking forward to it?"

"Yes. And that's a gross understatement."

"But you're not?" Cal asked.

"I'm anticipating having your mother all to myself for ten days and—"

Cal held up a hand. "Too much information, Dad."

His father grinned. "It's far too easy to mess with you. Not even a challenge."

Cal figured the bigger challenge was being married for so long. He'd always wanted what his parents had. They got it right with each other. He'd gone into his marriage to do the right thing, and instead turned into the biggest chump on the planet, suckered by the oldest con in the world—*I'm pregnant with your child.* Em was pregnant with his child and took him at his word when he'd adamantly declared ties and responsibilities were off limits for him. He smiled down at his daughter who was making a valiant effort not to fall asleep and figured he was eating those words now.

And not just because of Annie. He'd never gotten Emily out of his system even when they'd stopped seeing each other. The need for her lived inside him and had right from the beginning. It was more acute now than ever, but if he let her in knowing what she was capable of, he'd be worse than a chump.

"You know, Cal, I like that young woman. I always have."

He'd been hearing that a lot lately. "Okay."

"She was pretty upset when I saw her."

"Did she tell you what was wrong?"

"Multiple things. But I think what upset her most was feeling like she failed the teenager in her program."

He knew she'd taken the news of Patty's pregnancy pretty hard. He also knew she was tough and didn't wear her heart on her sleeve, so to confide in his dad wasn't like her. "You win some, you lose some."

"She's not responsible for the choices others make." Ken rested his elbows on his knees. "Only her own. She told me about the baby she gave up for adoption."

"Really?" The intensity of his tone disturbed Annie who'd just drifted off and he shushed and bounced her until she settled again, then looked at his father. "I'm surprised she told you about that."

"You make it sound as if she should be ashamed. In my opinion she showed courage, grace and dignity in an impossible situation. At fifteen and without family support there was no way for her to care for that child. A child she loved enough to give up. A child she'll think about and miss every day of her life. I think she paid a very high price for that mistake and it's not something I can hold against her."

"What about the mistake with me? The one where she didn't tell me that she was pregnant with my child. Your grandchild," Cal added.

"The way I understand it, you made it crystal clear that you wanted no strings attached. Looking at it from her perspective, and knowing how deeply she cares about people, I believe she was trying to do the right thing."

So not what Cal wanted to hear.

"You're saying it's my fault that she didn't come clean about the pregnancy?"

"I think your past has affected you to the point that you're painting every woman with a black brush."

"What's that supposed to mean?" When Annie stirred in her sleep again, Cal stood and carried her to the blanket he'd set on the floor. Mental note: He really needed to get a crib.

After putting his daughter down and soothing her until she quieted, he stood and motioned his father into the kitchen. "So you're saying I sabotage every social interaction with a woman because of what happened in my marriage?"

Ken leaned against the counter beside the refrigerator and crossed his arms over his chest. "Look, son, all I'm saying is that you might want to cut Emily some slack, and give yourself a break. She made a mistake but so did you."

"How?"

"Lori lied to you—"

"So did Em."

"It's not the same," his father said. "Your wife was a master of manipulation. She lied to get you to marry her. She faked suicide attempts to pressure you into not leaving her."

"You think I don't know the attempts were a cry for help? I needed to spend more time with her and work on the relationship."

"Which is exactly what she was counting on. If she'd been serious about killing herself, she'd have succeeded. It was emotional blackmail and worked brilliantly."

"Until she walked out," Cal said.

"Another way to hurt you." His father looked grim. "She understood your competitive nature. After all she was there in high school. The cheerleader watching the quarterback pull out all the stops to have an undefeated season. Leaving you when she'd exhausted all exploitation to prolong the marriage was clearly a way to get back at you, to keep you from getting a notch in the win column."

"What's your point, Dad?"

Ken blew out a long breath. "Your mother and I tried to teach you and Brad to always do the right thing."

"And?" Cal prompted.

"It backfired with you because of your tendency to be an overachiever who hates to lose. You take yourself out of play rather than risk failure."

"Are you trying to give Dr. Phil competition?" Cal said.

"Hardly." The older man smiled sadly. "I'm just pointing out that there's no such thing as perfect."

"You and mom practically are."

"We work at it, son. You don't see that. We've had our ups and downs. Don't get me wrong. There are more ups, but relationships aren't easy. The alternative is a series of unsatisfying social interactions. That sounds lonely and sad to me and I can't stand by and say nothing while your personal life is turning into a train wreck." Ken met his gaze. "Emily is the mother of your daughter."

"Not a newsflash." Cal didn't want to hear this. "Are you playing cupid, Dad? Because if you are, I gotta say that the costume doesn't look all that good on you."

"You're manufacturing a reason to keep Emily at arm's length. She's a remarkable woman."

"A regular Mother Teresa."

Ken put his hands on his hips. "She's not a saint, but why would you want that? The flaws are so much more interesting. Humanity is all about learning from mistakes and trying to do better. Believe me you could do far worse."

And he had, Cal thought. His father was right about one thing—he didn't want to repeat the failure. Was he right about the rest? That he refused to give the right one a chance because the wrong one had worked him over?

Em remarkable?

Definitely.

Hot?

Oh, yeah.

Had he already taken a big, emotional step with her without

realizing it? *Was* he in love with her? His father stopped short of saying that, but there was certainly some truth in everything else he'd said.

Em hit Cal's number on her cell phone speed dial and waited for him to pick up while the knots in her stomach knotted just a little tighter.

"Hello?"

The sound of his deep voice so strong and confident shouldn't be that wonderful to hear because it was the stuff of heart-break, but she couldn't stop the feeling. "Cal? It's Emily."

"I knew that. What with my caller ID and all. What's up?"

"I need a favor." She sat on her sofa and watched Annie toddle around the coffee table, trying to get the TV remote control that was just out of reach, then screech in frustration. Determination would be fantastic when she was an adult, but not so much now.

"What do you need?" Cal asked. There was no hint of sus-picion in his voice and that should count for something.

"Can I leave Annie with you? I know you're probably tired from working today, but—I wouldn't ask if it weren't important."

"I didn't work today and I'd love to keep Annie." Now sus-picion slipped into his tone. "You've got a date?"

"I wish." That remark made her into the liar he already believed her to be. He was the only man on the planet that she'd give her heart and soul to be with. "Patty and Henry are gone. I need to look for them."

"Gone? Where?"

She almost smiled. "If I knew the answer to that I wouldn't have to look."

"Okay. Right." The way he sounded now meant he was running his fingers through his hair. And probably pacing.

"She and Jonas had a big fight when she told him about the baby. He was pretty upset."

"Understandable."

"I agree. But now she and Henry are gone and he's frantic. He was going to skip work to look for them, but he can't afford to lose his job. I told him I'd go and keep him informed. So I'll bring Annie over and the portable crib because I'm not sure how long I'll be. It would be easier on her if you kept her overnight so—"

"I'll help you. We'll look together."

"You don't have to. If you could just take care of Annie. The places I'm going to look aren't anywhere I want to take her."

"Then you shouldn't go, either."

"I have to."

"Not alone. Pack her stuff. I'll pick you guys up and we'll take her to Mom and Dad's."

Before she could protest or ask how he knew his parents would be free or even want to watch Annie he hung up.

After dropping their daughter off with her ecstatic grandparents, Em sat in the front passenger seat of his SUV as they headed back across the valley toward old downtown Las Vegas.

"You didn't need to come with me," she protested, even though she wanted to kiss him for being there.

She wanted to kiss him for other things, too, but mostly for not letting her do this by herself. She knew all too well how "alone" felt and being with Cal was so much better. Also something she shouldn't count on or get used to because he'd made his feelings, or lack thereof, perfectly clear.

"Like I said before hanging up on you, I'm not letting you do this by yourself. Two pairs of eyes are better than one." He glanced over and headlights from passing cars revealed the concern in his eyes. "We're almost to the shelter, but if she's not there—do you have any other ideas where Patty would go? Maybe to her family?"

"I already called." Em hadn't thought it was possible, but her stomach knotted some more. "Her mother said that she hadn't heard from Patty and even if she had, she'd have told her one baby is bad enough, but two is ridiculous. She doesn't want anything to do with her or Henry. Then she called that sweet, innocent little boy an ugly name."

"Mother of the year. Not." His expression was grim. "My folks may drive me crazy with caring, but at least they *do* care. I can't imagine how Patty must feel."

"I can." She gripped her hands tightly together in her lap to keep from picking at her fingers, a nervous habit she'd finally conquered. "Talking to that mother, and I use the term loosely, brought back a lot of bad memories."

"I don't know what to say."

"You don't have to say anything." She met his gaze for a moment and smiled. "You're here. Show, don't tell. You don't talk the talk. You walk the walk. And I appreciate you being my friend."

"You're welcome." Cal glanced in the rearview mirror, then said, "So we're going to the homeless shelter?"

"It's where I first found her before bringing her to Helping Hands."

He exited the freeway then drove through one of the parts of town that the Office of Tourism didn't talk about. She saw people sitting in doorways or curbs with everything they owned in tattered backpacks or wire shopping carts.

The shelter was on Bridger Avenue and Fourth Street, not too far from the Clark County Justice Center. That seemed ironic when it felt like there was no justice in the world. It was dark and dirty and scary. At least when she'd been on the street, she'd been able to protect the baby inside her. Patty had two lives depending on her, and Em knew from personal experience how terrifying and awful it was. She prayed that Patty was somewhere safe.

After parking in front of the lighted building, Cal came around to her side of the car and opened the door. She slid out and looked around. People sat on the curb or bus bench. Some had nothing but a brown paper bag hiding a bottle inside that contained their poison of choice. Others looked with eyes vacant and hopeless. These were the ones who didn't get a roof over their head and a bed for the night. She remembered being one of those unlucky ones and the fear threatened to pull her under.

Standing beside the open car door Cal's big body blocked her in. "Em, what is it? You're shaking like the boogeyman is chasing you."

"He did once." It was still 80 degrees, but her teeth chattered. "I was fifteen and on the street and it was dark. Some guy tried to f-force himself on me."

"Em—" His jaw tightened. "Did you— Did he—"

"No. I kicked him, you know, and ran like hell."

"Attagirl." Resting his wrist on the top of the car he leaned down and met her gaze. "I can go in alone and look for her if it's too hard for you. But I don't want to leave you here by yourself."

And she didn't want to be left. "No. I'm okay."

He stood back and chirped the car locked after shutting the door. She started to step on the sidewalk when he stopped her and pulled her into his arms. The solid chest and warm skin were always safe and secure and satisfying, but felt especially wonderful right now. In the future, on cold and lonely nights the memory of this reassuring gesture and his solid presence would fill all the dark places in her soul. She slid her arms around his waist and held on. Just for a few moments.

She wanted so badly to pretend that he was here for *her*, that he cared about her for her sake and not just because she was his daughter's mother. But once upon a time she'd pretended that someone loved her. Instead he'd selfishly used her body and left her pregnant so that she ended up living on the streets. It had made her face reality and she'd promised herself to keep it real always.

Sighing, she stepped away and smiled up at him. "Thanks for that."

He nodded. "Let's go see if Patty's in there."

"Okay."

Before they could go inside, a movement from a doorway caught Em's attention. In the yellow glow from a streetlight there was a flash of blond hair followed by the cry of a child.

"Cal, over here." Ignoring the pleas for loose change from the few people on the sidewalk, she hurried to the doorway. In the shadows she saw a slight figure shrinking back with something in her arms. "Patty? It's Emily. Cal is with me."

"Em?" The teen stood and peeked out, then burst into tears.

Em pulled her and Henry into her arms and whispered comforting words, told her everything would be all right. Finally, Henry started to wiggle and slide out of her grasp.

Cal grabbed him into strong arms. "Hey, buddy, where do you think you're going?"

Patty sniffled and her lips trembled. "We don't have anywhere to go. By the time we got here the shelter was full and I couldn't get us in."

"You do have a place," Em told her firmly. "We're here to take you home."

"But I'm pregnant. Jonas said—" A sob choked off her words just before tears trickled down her cheeks and glistened in the glow from the streetlight.

"Jonas is worried sick about you and Henry," Cal said. "Stuff happens. To everyone. We all need help at one time or another. You can't take yourself out of the game."

"But I don't know how to make this better."

"And running away from the people who care about you is going to help?" Cal asked, sympathy in his eyes as he looked at Em. "You've got Lucy and Oscar. Emily. Me."

"You?" Patty said.

"I drove," he answered. "That makes me the leader of this rescue party. Jonas would have been here but he had to work. With another baby on the way he couldn't afford to jeopardize his job."

"I forgot. He wanted me to call if there was any news." Emily looked at the teen. "I'm going to let you do that."

Patty nodded and took the cell phone Em handed her. They moved a few feet away to give her some privacy while Henry yawned and put his head down on Cal's broad shoulder.

"I've been thinking," Cal said.

"That's encouraging. Although a little scary." Em studied him, her insides going all mushy at the sight of him with the small child in his strong arms.

"Right." He rested a wide palm on the boy's back. "Anyway, what do you think about signing Annie up for the convent?"

She knew he was trying to make her smile, right out here in the worst part of town. How heroic was he? And what harm could it do to go along with him.

"Right now?" she asked.

"Sure."

"I don't think it's like Little League sign-ups," she pointed out.

"It should be. Because the thought of her growing up and having to let her go is a pretty unpleasant thought. For the record I'm not in favor of her moving away from home until she's at least thirty-five. Although I hear they're always looking for candidates for the convent."

"Our daughter might have something to say about that," she pointed out.

"That doesn't mean we have to listen," he countered.

"Isn't it our job as parents to listen?" She glanced at Patty who was still talking on the cell. "My mom never did. I understand now what she was up against as a single woman raising a child and how difficult that is. And there's a good chance I wouldn't have gotten the message if she'd actually talked to me about it then. I was too young and self-absorbed. But she didn't try. More important, she didn't try to find out how I felt. She just told me how it was going to be and if I didn't like it, the door was right where it had always been."

"That's pretty harsh."

"Yeah. It was. But soon enough I found out the streets were a whole lot harsher. I'd never have gone back with my mom if there'd only been just me to worry about."

"I'm glad you took care of yourself. I'm glad you went home." His voice was rough, laced with emotion.

"Why? It meant giving up my baby. You made it clear how you felt about that."

"I talked the talk. But I didn't walk the walk that you did." He tightened his hold on Henry. "I'm sorry."

Her throat grew thick with emotion and she swallowed it back. "You don't have to say that. But thanks."

Patty finally hung up and told them that Jonas would meet her back at the apartment when he got off work. So the four of them got back into the SUV, with a sleeping Henry in Annie's car seat, and drove home.

Cal pulled up in front of her place and turned off the car. They walked Patty and Henry to the door where Lucy opened it.

The redhead hugged her friend. "I'm so glad you guys are safe."

Jonas took his son from Cal and hugged the sleeping boy, then put his arm around Patty. "You okay?"

"Yes." Patty nodded as tears filled her eyes. "Thanks to Em and Dr. Westen. Oh, Jonas— It was so awful. Henry was hungry and I didn't have any money to buy him food."

"Look, babe, I'm sorry. I acted like an ass. It was a shock, you know?" Jonas kept her close to his side. "But I didn't mean for you to run away. I don't know what I'd do without you guys."

"Really?" Patty blinked back more tears.

"Yeah. It'll be rough, but I know we can do it. Together." He looked at her. "I think we should get married."

"Now? But I thought you wanted to wait."

"That was before. Things have changed." He smiled down at her flat stomach.

"There's nothing I want more than to marry you." Patty smiled lovingly at him. "I know that means I'll have to leave Helping Hands, but it's time, I think. If I leave it will open up a place for someone who's all alone and doesn't have anywhere to go."

Em nodded as feelings crashed through her that she didn't have the emotional reserves to sort through right now. She promised the teens a long talk when they were all rested up, then Cal walked her to her place.

He took her key and fit it in the lock, then opened the door. "Hell of a night."

"That's an understatement."

"I guess there will be a wedding," he said.

"I guess." She took her keys from him and spotted her daughter's doll on the floor. The emptiness closed in on her. "Do you want to get Annie in the morning from your folks?"

"Yeah. Maybe we—"

She cut him off before he could ask to come in. "Thanks for that and for everything tonight. I appreciate it."

She couldn't let him stay because she wanted so badly for just that. Except they'd wind up in her bed and that would only put off the goodbye. The fact was that he couldn't give her his love and that was what she wanted more than anything.

"Good night, Cal."

Wordlessly he nodded and backed up, letting her shut the door. She leaned her back against it and listened to the deafening silence. She figured a place in hell was getting dusted off for her because of so many bad things she'd done, but mostly because she was jealous of the two teens who had each other. They were lucky. And she was happy for them, but so sad for herself.

Even walking the streets as a pregnant teenager with no place to go hadn't prepared her to be without Cal. She had never felt more alone than she did at this moment.

Chapter Fifteen

Emily watched Sophia take a bite of pepperoni-and-sausage pizza, then sigh with contentment. The other woman chewed enthusiastically and spoke with a full mouth. "There are very few things in life that pizza and wine can't fix."

"Or," Em said, "when you're full of carbs, fat and liquor you don't really care about the bad stuff."

"True." She wiped her mouth with a napkin. "Patty told me about her pregnancy, which explains her mood swings."

"She and Jonas are pulling together now."

"Legally speaking," Sophia said. "She invited me to the wedding."

"I'm a bridesmaid. Lucy's the maid of honor and Annie is going to be a flower girl," Em confirmed.

"All in all a lot of good things that don't require pizza and wine but we'll indulge anyway. Eat, drink and be merry."

Not so much. Emily looked at the generous slice on her

own plate and just sighed. It was barely touched and she couldn't work up a whole lot of enthusiasm to finish.

Her friend had called to suggest a girl's night in with wine and a whole lot of comfort food, the kind that would stick to their butts and thighs. Annie was spending the night at Cal's and Em hadn't wanted to be alone so she'd agreed. Now she wasn't so sure it was a good idea.

After setting her plate on the coffee table, Em said, "I'm sorry to be such pathetic company tonight."

"Thank God you finally said something." Sophia put her half-eaten pizza on the plate and set it aside. "My jaw is strained from smiling and talking. The cheerful act is starting to get on *my* nerves. You must be about ready to choke me."

"No, but now that you mention it—" Em grew serious and asked, "Why didn't you say something?"

"You'd have sidestepped me. Your favorite response when I ask what's going on is, and I quote—'oh, you know'—unquote." Sophia picked up her glass of red wine and sipped. "Are you ready to talk?"

"Same old, same old," she answered with a shrug.

"Something's different tonight." Sophia studied her as she tapped her glass to her lips. "It's like your spirit imploded."

"It feels like that."

"So what's changed?"

"I don't want to bring you down."

"Too late." Sophia met her gaze. "Spill it, my friend."

Emily hadn't planned to talk about this, figuring it would be best to keep things to herself, but the truth was her spirit was imploding and she didn't know how to stop it.

"Annie isn't just at Cal's tonight," she explained. "The Westens are having a party to celebrate that she's legally one of them. The paperwork is completed—signed, sealed, delivered and in the eyes of the world Cal is her father."

Em didn't need the paperwork for that to be true. Annie looked more like Cal every day and she knew that even if he'd never come back into her life she'd be reminded of him on a daily basis.

"So, why aren't you there with Annie instead of here bringing me down?" Sophia asked. "Did they not invite you?"

"No. Cal asked me to come. I just figured it would be best to stay away since it was my fault things happened the way they did in the first place."

"Then he didn't try very hard to let you know you were welcome."

"Actually, he told me he wasn't taking no for an answer, so I said something about not feeling well and keeping my germs to myself."

"You lied?"

"It got him to back off," she said, which neither confirmed or denied. Em slid into the corner of the couch and tucked one bare foot underneath her. "In his mind I was simply living up to his low expectations."

"You're telling me he's still got trust issues after you went to all the trouble of doing the court stuff to get him legal rights to his child?"

"He can't help it, Soph. I understand why."

"I don't. You're the most trustworthy person I know."

"Thanks for the vote of confidence."

"You're welcome." Her friend took another sip of red wine. "You haven't slept with him again."

"How do you know that?" Em cried. "Do I have a tattoo on my forehead? Is there a dialogue bubble over my head revealing my most private thoughts? What?"

"Your eyes are sad," Soph said simply.

"I hate that you know me so well."

"I hate that you're in love with him."

"Me, too." Em sat Indian style and faced her friend. "Samantha Tenney, his medical partner's wife, says that we're all broken in some way, but what doesn't kill us makes us stronger. I guess I'll have super powers by the time I get a handle on this."

"That's the spirit." Sophia nodded.

"The thing is that I feel like—I wish I could blame Cal, but—" To Em's horror, her throat closed with emotion and her eyes filled with tears. "I should be so happy that Annie has her family. She has people, and I only have her."

"You have Cal." Sophia put her glass on the table and moved forward.

"No, I don't."

"I beg to differ. He was there for you while you were going through that whole thing with the breast lump." She tapped her lip in thought. "And the time he stopped by after a bad day at work. That's proof of—something."

"Oh, yeah?" Em sniffled. "What would that be? He came to see Annie."

"He came to see his family. You. And Annie, too. But mostly you. You're his people. Whether he knows it or not, he cares about you."

"C-caring is a lot different from being in love with," Em pointed out, far too rationally considering this emotional meltdown.

She'd thought the pain of childbirth was a challenge but this soul-deep ache was far worse. Cal's past had broken something inside him and it couldn't be fixed. Her past had broken something in her that wouldn't let her risk his rejection and now he'd require a lie detector test to verify her honesty. *If only* were the two saddest words in the English language.

When two fat tears slipped from the corners of her eyes and rolled down her cheeks, Sophia swore in the most unladylike terms and gathered her close. "I'm going to give Cal Westen a piece of my mind."

"It won't do any good."

"It will do me a world of good," Sophia protested.

"How?"

"He needs to take his share of heat."

"He didn't do it on purpose."

"I don't care. There should be some payback for being the one who holds you when you cry over him."

Em laughed and cried and counted herself one of the lucky ones even though her heart was breaking. What had she done to deserve such unwavering friendship?

She also had her daughter. If she listed the pros and cons of her life, it would be heavy on the positive side. Maybe one of these days the pain wouldn't go so deep when Annie was with her father and Em was on the outside with her nose pressed up against the glass, looking at what she'd always wanted most and had let slip through her fingers.

It was the beginning of September and the thermometer was still registering in the triple digits but Emily couldn't wait for fall—Halloween and dressing Annie up in a costume, Thanksgiving and turkey. Christmas with presents and watching her daughter rip into them. She and Cal were going to have to figure out which of them she was going to spend the holiday with—just like a divorced couple with a child, except they'd never been married.

She'd just put her little girl to bed and was trying to figure out whether to mop the kitchen floor or clean out the refrigerator when there was a knock on the door. Her heart jumped because it was unusual at this time of night. But the thought that Cal might have stopped by really got her ticker kicking.

She peeked through the peephole and tried not to feel disappointed because Patty stood there. After opening, she said, "Hi."

Jonas was behind his fiancée. "Sorry to bother you. It's getting late, but we couldn't wait to tell you."

"Okay," she said, standing back to let them in.

Patty was practically vibrating with excitement. "We're moving out."

Em turned the deadbolt. "Really? Are you sure that's a good idea? Waiting just a little while would let you guys save some money and with the baby on the way—"

"The place we're getting won't cost us much," Jonas said. "And it's a house."

"I don't understand." Em crossed her arms over her chest. "Is there some kind of housing grant or a program I'm not aware of?"

Patty looked at her guy. "It's called the Cal Westen housing plan for teen parents with initiative."

"I don't understand."

"Dr. Westen bought a house and is going to let us use it for twenty-five dollars a month until Jonas finishes school and gets a good job."

Em could feel her jaw drop as she stared at them. "I don't know what to say."

"We thought he was kidding," Patty said. "He wasn't, and said we should consider it part of the Westen wedding gifting."

"His words," Jonas added. He put his arm around Patty. "So a week from now we'll be married and have a house. With a yard for the kids."

"That's wonderful." Em smiled at them. "I expect to be invited to the housewarming."

"You'll be the second person on the list," Patty told her.

"Dr. Westen is first. He called me earlier but Patty wanted us to tell you together and I just got off work." Jonas grinned.

Actually he hadn't stopped since the door opened. "We have to get back because Lucy's watching Henry, but we wanted to share the good news."

Em walked them to the door. "This is wonderful. I'm so happy for you guys. Really."

"Me, too." Patty hugged her. "It's just like you said, Em. Things have a way of working out."

For some, Em thought after she'd closed the door. Others were destined to make mistakes and live with the fallout. And that was possibly the most pathetic thought she'd ever had. No time like the present to stop feeling sorry for herself. Before she could figure out how to do that, there was another knock. Patty and Jonas probably forgot to tell her something.

She opened the door and Cal stood there. Her heart kicked up again and it would be a miracle if he couldn't hear it. "Hi."

"Hey," he said. "Can I come in?"

She didn't remember him saying he was going to stop by and that's something she wasn't likely to forget, what with being in love with him and all. That meant this wasn't planned, which meant— "Is everything all right?"

"Yeah. I just needed to see you."

"Annie, you mean," she clarified. "You wanted to make sure your daughter is all right."

He shook his head. "I meant you."

Wow. "I'm fine, and so is Annie. She's asleep, but you're welcome to see her. Anytime." She stepped back so he could come in.

"Thanks, Em." He walked past her and into Annie's bedroom where he pulled the light blanket over her chubby legs. After dropping a soft kiss on her forehead, he followed Em into the living room.

She twisted her fingers together. "Actually I'm glad you stopped by. There's something I wanted to discuss with you."

"Me, too." He frowned and folded his arms over his chest. "You first."

"I was thinking that Fall is just around the corner. Now that all your legal rights as her father are in place, I thought we should decide how to divide up where Annie spends the holidays."

"I don't want to give up any time with her."

Em's stomach knotted. "Silly me for thinking anything had changed simply because you decided to help Patty and Jonas with housing."

"They told you?"

"Just a little while ago. It's very nice of you, by the way." She wanted to hate him, but couldn't manage it.

"I didn't do it to be nice."

"Oh?"

"I've been lucky with my relatives, so I've taken some things for granted. Lately it's come to my attention that the definition of family is more than just the people who share your DNA." He looked down at her. "Those two kids feel like part of my family."

That capacity to care was just one of the many things to love about Cal Westen. How she'd misjudged him.

"You've really changed your tune from the day you wanted me to turn my back on Helping Hands and this neighborhood because it wasn't the right environment for Annie."

"Yeah." He looked uncomfortable. "It turns out I learned a lot from your next-door neighbors. Jonas showed me what it means to 'man up' and quit running away."

"He's a good kid."

"So is Patty," he agreed. "With a little support they'll have a great start to building their future."

"Yeah." It's what she was trying to do. Move on. Not easy, but she'd pulled off hard stuff before. Which brought her back to more hard stuff—the fact that Cal didn't want to share his daughter for the holidays. "Now that you know about Annie it won't be easy to not have her on a holiday, but we have to agree—"

"I'm not finished yet."

"Oh." That was too bad because she so wanted this painful face-to-face to be over.

"I've made so many mistakes with you."

"You have?" That got her attention. He had it the moment she'd seen him in the doorway, but now he *really* had it.

"I tried to forget you when you dumped me." She opened her mouth to protest, but he held up his hand. "I understand now. You had no reason to believe that the man who was renouncing commitment would treat you any differently than your mother."

Em stared up at him, hoping this wasn't a dream. "So you're not painting me with the liar's brush anymore?"

"You have the purest heart I've ever known." He stared at her. "You take responsibility for your actions and would do anything for the people you care about. When Patty ran away you'd have moved heaven and earth to find her. I wish I had half your heart."

"You do, Cal. What you're doing for those kids is extraordinary."

"It's selfish. I did it to get your attention. To show you I understand the meaning of commitment. And to get you to give me another chance." He ran his fingers through his hair. "The first time I saw you, I fell in love with you. Then you broke things off. It wasn't about who walked away first, it was about you taking my heart when you left. That hurt more than anything and I didn't ever want to feel that way again. So I dated. A lot. As Rhonda so eloquently put it, I got older but the women I went out with didn't."

Em really didn't want to hear about other women in his life. "You don't need to tell me this."

"I need to tell it." He rested his hands on his lean hips. "The day you walked back into my life, I fell for you all over again and it scared the crap out of me. I used anything and everything to push you away. Believe me, I know what an idiot I've been."

Em had never expected to hear any of this from him and joy surged through her. "Cal, I don't—"

He held up a hand to stop her. "I promise to never let you down again. And I'd like it very much if you'd marry me, but I understand if you can't bring yourself to believe in me."

"I— That's really— Wow, you don't beat around the bush, do you."

"Not when I want something."

"You want me?" she asked.

"Oh, yeah." There was a question in his eyes. "Do you love me? I understand if you can't."

"If I said no it would be a lie."

"So that's a yes, no?" he asked.

"It's a yes, yes." She started laughing and he gathered her into his arms.

The corners of his mouth curved up and love sparkled in his eyes. "You've set a high bar for honest and straightforward, so it would be best to start our life together on a truthful note. I would never understand or accept a no to my proposal. I'd already planned to just hang around until you changed your mind. I'm not willing to lose you again because I'm too much of a coward to take a chance." Intensity hummed through him. "Marry me, Em. Make me the happiest man in the world. Give me the family I've always wanted."

"How could I say no when that's everything I've always wanted?" she asked, trembling with all the feelings that were too big to put into words. It seemed too simple, and at the same time completely right. "I love you so much, Cal. There's nothing that would make me happier than marrying you."

He cupped her face in his hands and kissed her softly before saying, "I'm going to hold you to that."

"And I'm just going to hold you." She slid her arms around him and rested her cheek on his chest. "On one condition."

"Anything."

"Do I have to move into your house after we're married?" she asked.

"I was sort of counting on you and Annie living with me." He held her away from him and met her gaze. "You're worried about Helping Hands."

"Yes, but I think I know someone who'd be perfect for it." It was so wonderful how well he understood her. "You haven't met Sophia yet, and when you do she might be a little hostile at first. She'll get over it."

"If you like her I'll like her," he promised.

"I know you will. And she doesn't know it yet, but this apartment is going to be her new home." Em looked around and knew she would miss this place. "I hope it brings her as much happiness as it's brought me."

"And me," Cal said.

Then he lowered his mouth to hers again and took care of showing her all the tenderness and love she'd longed for her whole life. The only thing that could make her happier was a brother or sister for Annie. Another baby for her and the doctor would make life just about perfect.

* * * * *

*Celebrate 60 years of pure
reading pleasure with Harlequin!*

To commemorate the event, Harlequin Intrigue® is
thrilled to invite you to the wedding of The Colby
Agency's J. T. Baxley and his bride, Eve Mattson.

That is, of course, if J.T. can find the woman who left
him at the altar. Considering he's a private investigator
for one of the top agencies in the country—the best of
the best—that shouldn't be a problem. The real setback
is that his bride isn't who she appears to be…and her
mysterious past has put them both in danger.

*Enjoy an exclusive glimpse of Debra Webb's
latest addition to*
**THE COLBY AGENCY:
ELITE RECONNAISSANCE DIVISION**

THE BRIDE'S SECRETS

*Available August 2009
from Harlequin Intrigue®.*

The dark figures on the dock were still firing. The bullets cutting through the surface of the water without the warning boom of shots told Eve they were using silencers.

That was to her benefit. Silencers decreased the accuracy of every shot and lessened the range.

She grabbed for the rocks. Scrambled through the darkness. Bumped her knee on a boulder. Cursed.

Burrowing into the waist-deep grass, she kept low and crawled forward. Faster. Pushed harder. Needed as much distance as possible.

Shots pinged on the rocks.

J.T. scrambled alongside her.

He was breathing hard.

They had to stay close to the ground until they reached the next row of warehouses. Even though she was relatively certain they were out of range at this point, she wasn't taking any risks. And she wasn't slowing down.

J.T. had to keep up.

The splat of a bullet hitting the ground next to Eve had her rolling left. Maybe they weren't completely out of range.

She bumped J.T. He grunted.

His injured arm. Dammit. She could apologize later.

Half a dozen more yards.

Almost in the clear.

As she reached the cover of the alley between the first two warehouses she tensed.

Silence.

No pings or splats.

She glanced back at the dock. Deserted.

Time to run.

Her car was parked another block down.

Pushing to her feet, she sprinted forward. The wet bag dragged at her shoulder. She ignored it.

By the time she reached the lot where her car was parked, she had dug the keys from her pocket and hit the fob. Six seconds later she was behind the wheel. She hit the ignition as J.T. collapsed into the passenger seat. Tires squealed as she spun out of the slot.

"What the hell did you do to me?"

From the corner of her eye she watched him shake his head in an attempt to clear it.

He would be pissed when she told him about the tranquilizer.

She'd needed him cooperative until she formulated a plan. A drug-induced state of unconsciousness had been the fastest and most efficient method to ensure his continued solidarity.

"I can't really talk right now." Eve weaved into the right lane as the street widened to four lanes. What she needed was traffic. It was Saturday night—shouldn't be that difficult to find as soon as they were out of the old warehouse district.

A glance in the rearview mirror warned that their unwanted company had caught up.

Sensing her tension, J.T. turned to peer over his left shoulder.

"I hope you have a plan B."

She shot him a look. "There's always plan G." Then she pulled the Glock out of her waistband.

Cutting the steering wheel left, she slid between two vehicles. Another veer to the right and she'd put several cars between hers and the enemy.

She was betting they wouldn't pull out the firepower in the open like this, but a girl could never be too sure when it came to an unknown enemy.

Deep blending was the way to go.

Two traffic lights ahead the marquis of a movie theater provided exactly the opportunity she was looking for.

The digital numbers on the dash indicated it was just past midnight. Perfect timing. The late movie would be purging its audience into the crowd of teenagers who liked hanging out in the parking lot.

She took a hard right onto the property that sported a twelve-screen theater, numerous fast-food hot spots and a chain superstore. Speeding across the lot, she selected a lane of parking slots. Pulling in as close to the theater entrance as possible, she shut off the engine and reached for her door.

"Let's go."

Thankfully he didn't argue.

Rounding the hood of her car, she shoved the Glock into her bag, then wrapped her arm around J.T.'s and merged into the crowd.

With her free hand she finger-combed her long hair. It was soaked, as were her clothes. The kids she bumped into noticed, gave her death-ray glares.

They just didn't know.

As she and J.T. moved in closer to the building, she grabbed a baseball cap from an innocent bystander. The crowd made it easy. The kid who owned the cap had made it even easier by stuffing the cap bill-first into his waistband at the small of his back.

Pushing through the loitering crowd, she made her way to the side of the building next to the main entrance. She pushed J.T. against the wall and dropped her bag to the ground. Peeled off her tee and let it fall.

His gaze instantly zeroed in on her breasts, where the cami she wore had glued to her skin like an extra layer. A zing of desire shot through her veins.

Not the time.

With a flick of her wrist she twisted her hair up and clamped the cap atop the blond mass.

"They're coming," J.T. muttered as he gazed at some point beyond her.

"Yeah, I know." She planted her palms against the wall on either side of him and leaned in. "Keep your eyes open. Let me know when they're inside."

Then she planted her lips on his.

* * * * *

Will J.T. and Eve be caught in the moment?
Or will Eve get the chance to reveal all of her secrets?
Find out in
THE BRIDE'S SECRETS
by Debra Webb
Available August 2009 from Harlequin Intrigue®

We'll be spotlighting a different series every month
throughout 2009 to celebrate our 60th anniversary.

LOOK FOR
HARLEQUIN INTRIGUE®
IN AUGUST!

To commemorate the event, Harlequin Intrigue® is thrilled
to invite you to the wedding of the Colby Agency's
J. T. Baxley and his bride, Eve Mattson.

Look for *Colby Agency: Elite Reconnaissance*

THE BRIDE'S SECRETS
BY DEBRA WEBB

Available August 2009

www.eHarlequin.com

REQUEST YOUR FREE BOOKS!

2 FREE NOVELS PLUS 2 FREE GIFTS!

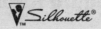

SPECIAL EDITION®

Life, Love and Family!

YES! Please send me 2 FREE Silhouette Special Edition® novels and my 2 FREE gifts (gifts are worth about $10). After receiving them, if I don't wish to receive any more books, I can return the shipping statement marked "cancel." If I don't cancel, I will receive 6 brand-new novels every month and be billed just $4.24 per book in the U.S. or $4.99 per book in Canada. That's a savings of at least 15% off the cover price! It's quite a bargain! Shipping and handling is just 50¢ per book.* I understand that accepting the 2 free books and gifts places me under no obligation to buy anything. I can always return a shipment and cancel at any time. Even if I never buy another book from Silhouette, the two free books and gifts are mine to keep forever.

235 SDN EYN4   335 SDN EYPG

Name _____ (PLEASE PRINT)

Address _____ Apt. #

City _____ State/Prov. _____ Zip/Postal Code

Signature (if under 18, a parent or guardian must sign)

Mail to the **Silhouette Reader Service:**
IN U.S.A.: P.O. Box 1867, Buffalo, NY 14240-1867
IN CANADA: P.O. Box 609, Fort Erie, Ontario L2A 5X3

Not valid to current subscribers of Silhouette Special Edition books.

**Want to try two free books from another line?
Call 1-800-873-8635 or visit www.morefreebooks.com.**

* Terms and prices subject to change without notice. Prices do not include applicable taxes. Sales tax applicable in N.Y. Canadian residents will be charged applicable provincial taxes and GST. Offer not valid in Quebec. This offer is limited to one order per household. All orders subject to approval. Credit or debit balances in a customer's account(s) may be offset by any other outstanding balance owed by or to the customer. Please allow 4 to 6 weeks for delivery. Offer available while quantities last.

Your Privacy: Silhouette is committed to protecting your privacy. Our Privacy Policy is available online at www.eHarlequin.com or upon request from the Reader Service. From time to time we make our lists of customers available to reputable third parties who may have a product or service of interest to you. If you would prefer we not share your name and address, please check here. ☐

SSE09R

Stay up-to-date on all your romance reading news!

The Harlequin Inside Romance newsletter is a **FREE** quarterly newsletter highlighting our upcoming series releases and promotions!

Go to
eHarlequin.com/InsideRomance
or e-mail us at
InsideRomance@Harlequin.com
to sign up to receive
your FREE newsletter today!